A former job-hopper, **Jessica Lemmon** resides in Ohio with her husband and rescue dog. She holds a degree in graphic design, which is currently gathering dust in an impressive frame. When she's not writing supersexy heroes, she can be found cooking, drawing, drinking coffee (okay, wine) and eating crisps. She firmly believes that God gifts us with talents for a purpose, and with His help, you can create the life you want.

Jessica is a social media junkie who loves to hear from readers. You can learn more at jessicalemmon.com.

Also by Jessica Lemmon

Dynasties: Beaumont Bay

Second Chance Love Song
Good Twin Gone Country

The Dunn Brothers

Million-Dollar Mix-Up
Million-Dollar Consequences

Texas Cattleman's Club

An Ex to Remember
The Man She Loves to Hate

Discover more at millsandboon.co.uk.

The Man She Loves to Hate

JESSICA LEMMON

MILLS & BOON

First published in Great Britain 2023
by Mills & Boon, an imprint of HarperCollins*Publishers* Ltd,
1 London Bridge Street, London, SE1 9GF

www.harpercollins.co.uk

HarperCollins*Publishers*
Macken House, 39/40 Mayor Street Upper,
Dublin 1, D01 C9W8, Ireland

Large Print edition 2023

Special thanks and acknowledgement
are given to Jessica Lemmon for her contribution to the
Texas Cattleman's Club: The Wedding miniseries.

ISBN: 978-0-263-31266-9

06/23

This book is produced from independently certified FSC™ paper
to ensure responsible forest management.
For more information visit www.harpercollins.co.uk/green.

Printed and Bound in the UK using 100% Renewable Electricity
at CPI Group (UK) Ltd, Croydon, CR0 4YY

One

For the last three years, Rylee Meadows had been planning weddings for high profile, wealthy clients. Those clients had ranged from celebrities to regular old rich folks. Special requests were not outside of the norm, nor were last-minute changes. But this was the first time she'd ever had to contend with a wedding *crasher*.

The wedding of Xavier Noble and Ariana Ramos was coming up in a few days. Reaching this point had required Herculean effort. Not only on Rylee's part, but on the parts of the vendors who had been tasked with pulling off nothing short of perfection while navigating a sea of difficulties—including the blackout that had affected half of the town of Royal, Texas.

As a professional used to high-pressure situations, Rylee could have rolled with the blackout alone and not broken a sweat, save for that *other* anomaly keeping everyone involved in this wedding on their toes.

His name? Patrick “Trick” MacArthur.

Trick—oh, how appropriate—was a social media star who’d grown famous for crashing events which he had not been invited to. Right now, his sights were set on the Noble-Ramos wedding.

After all Rylee and the hardworking, talented vendors had been through with planning this wedding, a troublemaker in town was the last thing any of them needed.

Xavier and Ariana had entrusted her with facilitating the perfect day for them, and Rylee wouldn’t let them down. However, it had become apparent that Trick, who had taken up residence close by, wasn’t going anywhere. The man had made a living showing up where he wasn’t invited, which had pushed more than one of her buttons.

In the past, Rylee had been accused of being a bit of a perfectionist. She understood why. She was used to having complete control of her environment. Trick's presence at the wedding, and reception, could ruin the day for everyone. She could not, and would not allow it.

She'd done her research, and while she could objectively understand Patrick's appeal, she couldn't support his antics. One look at any of his online videos revealed an engaging, smiling man one might describe as the life of the party. He was great-looking, with thick black hair that beckoned a woman's fingers, hazel eyes that held enough mischief to be intriguing, and a seemingly permanent smirk surrounded by sexy stubble.

Rylee grunted as she parked her car on the curb. She'd never been drawn in by a bad boy type, and had no plans on starting now. She'd tracked down Trick to this very tailor in order to corner him and make him a proposition. If he wouldn't willingly leave Royal, then he would have to agree to stay within the boundary lines she drew. Once she'd convinced him to behave himself, she would approach the bride and groom and explain how this was the way—the only way—to move forward.

She stepped onto the curb, wincing as she walked toward the crosswalk. *These damn shoes.* Gingerly, she slipped the strap from her foot to find a blister forming. She sat on a nearby park bench and pulled the emergency bridal kit from her bag.

She'd learned a long time ago not to show up at a wedding, or anywhere, really, *without* bandages or bobby pins. As she planned weddings and similar "emergencies" arose, she'd added to the kit. Now she carried acid reducers, aspirin and a miniature sewing kit, among other items a panicky bride might need. Or in this case, the bride's harried wedding planner.

Band-Aid in place, she rolled her shoulders, and tucked a strand of hair back into her coiffed chignon. The day had been a long one, and she'd skipped dinner to iron out an issue with the outdoor seating plan. Thankfully this was her last stop for the day, and bonus, Trick wasn't expecting her. She'd crash *his* appointment and see how he liked it.

With a satisfied smile on her face—she

loved it when a plan came together—she entered the shop packed with designer suits, ties, shirts and shoes. Glass cases containing cufflinks, watches and jewelry lined the back wall, a familiar sight. She'd been in this shop countless times to help the groom choose the proper wardrobe for his big day.

At the counter, she waved hello to Harold, who was shining the glass with a cloth.

"Rylee." He smiled and offered his hand, which she took and shook cordially. "You're working late."

"I'm here to see one of your customers, actually. I assume Shayla is with him?" Shayla was a tailor and a damn good one. She had an eye for detail. It wasn't a typical career choice for a gorgeous thirty-two-year-old woman, but Royal was a unique place with unique residents.

"In the back," Harold answered. "Help yourself."

"Thanks, I will." Rylee adjusted her purse on her shoulder and strode into the back room where she encountered Shayla and Patrick. Shayla, dressed in her usual button-down pale blue shirt and trousers, a pin cushion strapped to her wrist, was focused on his suit jacket. Patrick, who caught sight of Rylee in the mirror he faced, was wearing a lot less.

A slow grin spread his lips. The eye contact was intense, sending a drove of gooseflesh to crop up on Rylee's bare arms. The flush on her neck and cheeks had come thanks to what was so obviously missing.

His pants.

"Well, well, if it isn't Rylee Meadows," Patrick said, his gaze unerringly on her reflection.

Shayla lifted her head to offer a casual, "Oh, hey, Rye. We're almost done here and then I can help you with whatever you need."

Rylee snapped her attention from Patrick's bare legs and slouched black socks, accidentally admiring his calf muscles and the scant dark, wiry hair on his strong thighs that disappeared beneath his currently-being-pinned suit jacket. Some part of her she'd rather not acknowledge was disappointed at not having a view of his butt. She shut her eyes to reset her very tired brain.

"I'm, uh, I'm here to talk to Trick. Patrick. Mr. MacArthur."

He looked over his shoulder at her, one dark eyebrow winging upward. "Please don't call me Mr. MacArthur. It makes me feel geriatric."

Shayla laughed as she gave him a once-over. "You're looking good to me. Ready to lose the jacket?" Shayla sent a rogue look over at Rylee. "And put on some pants so you don't fluster Ms. Meadows any more than you already have?"

"I'm fairly certain Ms. Meadows is un-fluster-able."

"I'm fairly certain you are right." Shayla collected the suit pants set aside on a chair and then waited for him to slip off the suit jacket. She palmed Rylee's shoulder on her way out of the room. "Take your time."

Patrick pulled on a pair of trousers. Rylee watched long enough to discern that he was a boxer-briefs guy with a decent-looking butt, before turning her back and granting him the privacy he hadn't bothered asking for.

"Did you come in to check me out, or is this a professional visit?" he asked, reminding her that wherever he was involved, it was destined to be an uphill climb.

"I have a proposition for you, Mr.—uh, Patrick."

"Trick is fine, Rye."

"It's Rylee to you." She spun around to find him cinching his belt. He wore a white button-down shirt, the collar open to reveal an attractive neck. He stood tall, confident despite not wearing any shoes, as confident as he'd been previously while not wearing any pants. Even so, he struck her as trustworthy and safe, a bizarre assessment given her reason for being here tonight. The infamous Trick MacArthur was known for being disingenuous and opportunistic. The thought caused her eyebrows to meet over her nose.

"Okay. Rylee." He sat on a footstool and slipped on a pair of leather loafers, Italian leather if she wasn't mistaken, and then stood again. As you say in Texas, "What can I do ya for?"

"I'm not sure that saying derived from Texas."

He frowned. "No?"

"No." She straightened her back. "But I am fairly certain that *This ain't my first rodeo* did. Which brings me to the reason for my visit."

"Are you asking me to go to a rodeo with you?"

She ignored the question. "I'm here to make a bargain with you before you cause a ruckus at Xavier and Ariana's wedding."

"A ruckus?" He approached, enveloping her in a bouquet of familiar scents. Bergamot, mandarin and fruity but also peppery.

"Dior Sauvage?" she blurted. Startled by her own outburst, she blinked. "Your cologne. I have a weird talent for guessing men's colognes. A talent I've fostered for the grooms in the weddings I plan," she continued blathering. "Most of the time they don't know what they like, and want something special but not overpowering for the big day. Anyway, never mind."

"I'm impressed. Dior is my go-to."

It suited him. The fragrance was complex. One part bad-boy, one part sophistication. Trick managed to pull off both. The scent was subtle, as if he'd sprayed it on this morning and the fragrance had lessoned as the hours had ticked by. A vision of him stepping out of the shower, water rivulets trickling off his bare chest and over the curve of his round butt invaded her imagination. By the time he was pushing a hand through wet hair and wiping the steam off a mirror, she'd completely lost her place.

"Your proposition?" he prompted.

Right. That.

"I assume you'd like to attend the Noble-Ramos wedding."

His head jerked on his neck. "Are you offering me an invitation?"

"Sort of. As you know Xavier and Ariana are America's favorite couple at the moment."

"Hence my presence here in the great state of Texas." He spread his arms, his toothy grin sharklike, but no less attractive. What must it be like not to worry about anyone but yourself? Rylee worried about everyone else most of the time. Then again, she was in the service industry and Trick…was not.

"If I give you ample access to the final preparations for the wedding, you will be able to film, at your discretion, all of what happens up and until the actual wedding and reception." She hoped that his pursed lips and narrowed eyes were signs he was considering her offer.

"What's the catch?"

"You are prohibited from filming the wedding or reception, though you are welcome to attend as an *invited* guest."

"And…?" he asked as if he'd sensed there was more. He was right.

"*And* you will be asked to donate the revenue for any monetized videos to a charity of Xavier's and Ariana's choosing."

"Done."

"Hear me out before you…" Her tired brain belatedly processed his easy acquiescence. "Excuse me?"

"It's a deal." He held out his hand for her to shake. She regarded it skeptically. "Come on, Rylee. This is why you're here. What are you waiting for?" He flipped his hand so that it was palm up. "Seal the deal."

"Now I'm waiting for the catch."

"You think there's a catch?" His smile hinted at that very probability.

She had five days to pull off this wedding and he was being ten times more agreeable than she could have hoped. She'd ambushed him. She had expected, and was ready for, a fight. He'd been planning to disrupt this wedding for months, and instead of fighting with her, he was in agreement with her.

She wasn't sure she could trust him, but what choice did she have? She placed her hand in his.

He gripped her firmly. "If—"

"Oh, come on."

"—you have dinner with me tonight. I'm starving."

She opened her mouth to refuse him, but before a single word exited her lips, her stomach growled audibly.

Trick chuckled, the warmth of his touch sliding up her arm and curling around her in an entirely comfortable way. He leaned in closer. So close, she could make out each individual hair on his jawline, and the gold flecks dancing in his hazel eyes. His lips parted, his gaze locked with hers…

"That sounds like a yes to me, Rylee Meadows," he murmured before letting go of her. Then he clapped his hands and rubbed them together. "Where's the best sloppy cheeseburger in town?"

Two

The obvious choice for a burger was the Royal diner, but Rylee didn't trust Trick in such a casual atmosphere. The mere thought of him bantering with the waitress and lounging in the red faux leather booths set her teeth on edge. She didn't need a challenge tonight. She needed a cocktail.

She handed off the key fob for her borrowed Mercedes to the valet. As she accepted her ticket, Patrick came around to stand behind her.

"Thanks for driving." He took in the brick exterior and the traditional signage of the restaurant.

"No problem." Her manners had insisted.

"Shall we?" He offered an arm, which was far more gentlemanly than she would have expected from him. Rather than argue, as dinner was a condition of their freshly minted agreement, she rested her hand on his forearm and allowed him to lead her inside.

Despite the late hour, the restaurant was fairly busy. Not surprising considering the amount of business and pleasure being conducted in town. She would bet there were plenty of opportunists—in addition to Trick—who'd traveled to town to report on the Noble-Ramos wedding.

"The RCW Steakhouse is owned by Rafe Cortez-Williams," she told Trick as the hostess led them to a table. "The beef they serve comes straight from the family's cattle ranch."

"Impressive."

Once they were seated and large leather-bound menus were handed to each of them, he looked around. She joined him. The table and chairs were made of rich, dark wood, the windows framed by heavy drapes. The style was traditional, but she found the decor soothing rather than stodgy. She'd been born into affluent wealth and was accustomed to country-club chic, in its varying forms.

"This is cozy. I thought you'd opt for a brightly lit diner, but instead you've tucked me into a sensual, shadowed corner." His lips flinched, the smirk at home on his face.

"You said sloppy burger." She casually scanned the menu. "No one does it better than RCW. Not even the diner."

"Unpopular opinion?"

"Completely. But I'm an uppity rich girl, so you get what you get." She slapped the menu closed. She didn't consider herself "uppity," but she knew plenty of people who described her family that way. She'd been accused of being particular, a perfectionist and rigid. Her ex-fiancé had labeled her as "too ambitious" before he ended their engagement.

Their waiter arrived and Rylee and Trick put in their food order. He chose a burger with fried onions, pickles and American cheese and she opted for the same, only she added bacon to hers.

"You're brave," he said when the waiter left.

"Not used to a woman ordering a cheeseburger?"

"Not one dressed in a buttercream silk dress. You look beautiful in that color, by the way."

Taken aback by the compliment, she tucked a stray lock of pale blond hair behind her ear. "I'm probably wilting at this point. My hair is falling, my dress is wrinkled. These shoes are well past their expiration date."

He bent to look beneath the table at her feet. "Those straps seem painful."

"They are."

"Why do you wear them?"

She laughed. "Because Converse sneakers would be inappropriate with this dress?"

He nodded, but appeared thoughtful. She didn't know much about Patrick beyond the rumors that had preceded his visit to town. Now that they were here, as he'd said in this "shadowed" corner, the setting *did* feel intimate. Her polite upbringing required cordiality, and so she dipped her toe into well-worn territory: small talk.

"Why weddings?"

"Why…weddings?" he repeated.

"Yes. Why do you crash weddings and film them?" She sipped from her water glass.

"It's not always weddings. I've crashed a few private concerts, birthday parties in Beverly Hills. At least one awards show."

"I saw that one. You were escorted out by security and ended up running from the cops. Classy."

"That was a long time ago." He averted his eyes like he wasn't proud of his past.

"Yes, but you're here *now*. Planning hijinks for the Noble-Ramos wedding. Clearly, you're not reformed."

"Hijinks? That's quite the Scooby-Doo description of my career."

"A career made of showing up where no one wants you?"

He didn't crumble beneath the veiled insult, but smiled and leaned back in his chair instead. He tapped the end of his salad fork on the table lightly as he spoke. "When I was younger, my college friends and I pulled a lot of dumb shit on unsuspecting people. Nothing malicious."

"I've seen a few of those older videos. In one of them, you replaced the speaker at a fast-food restaurant with your own and whenever someone pulled up, you sang a popular song and goaded them into joining you." Watching the unsuspecting person in the car laugh as they eventually sang along *was* entertaining, and had the surprising biproduct of making her feel light and happy.

"You've done your research."

"You didn't give me much of a choice. It's good to know one's adversary."

"Is that what we are? I thought we just became partners."

The waiter delivered their burgers and asked if they needed anything else. Trick waited for Rylee to answer, and when she said *no, thank you*, he followed suit. Charming and polite. How totally unexpected.

They each lifted their burgers, their gazes locking for one charged second before she took her first bite. Juicy, flavorful, tender meat and a butter-brushed Brioche bun was offset by the crunch of lettuce, onions, bacon and pickles in between. The burger was heaven, and drew a low groan of approval from her throat.

He set down his burger and swiped his mouth with the black cloth napkin, nodding as he chewed.

"Damn," he said as soon as his mouth wasn't full. *"Damn."*

"Good, right?" Holding her burger in one hand, Rylee dabbed her lips with her own napkin before taking another bite.

One "damn" had been for how good the burger tasted, the other reserved for Rylee. Her fair blond hair was pulled back, revealing the creamy expanse of her neck. One thin strap of her dress had slipped ever so slightly off her shoulder, and then she'd buried her face into her burger and had taken a hearty bite.

She was exquisite.

He couldn't remember being as enamored by anyone as much as he was by her right now—and he was a guy who noticed the little things. Who noticed nearly everything.

He'd seen her around since he'd arrived in town. The second he'd laid eyes on the take-charge, in-charge, unflappable wedding planner, he'd been smitten. He liked her sass and her professional attitude as much as he liked the way she looked. He liked how tall she was, the way her curves tested the seams of the classy dresses she wore. The way her blue eyes sought him out in earnest, like she was trying to figure him out…

Especially that last part.

When she'd caught him with his pants literally down tonight, he'd been instantly glad to see her.

The friends he used to film videos with had graduated and gone on to lucrative careers. Trick had built an empire without meaning to, and in three short years. He'd landed sponsorships when his social channel's numbers began hitting six digits, and now he was well into the sevens. It wasn't a traditional career path, that was for damn sure. He'd attended film school and had been certain he'd be an intern on a movie set by now, begging for ten seconds with the director so he could pitch his own movie ideas.

"Partners, huh?" she asked out of the blue. Funny, he'd assumed she'd been anxious to change the subject.

"You need me to film the pre-show. I agreed."

"First of all, I don't *need* you to film anything. I'm trying to corral you."

"Many women have tried that tack before, Rylee." He grinned.

"How many?" She raised her fair eyebrows in challenge.

"Not *that* many." He didn't want her thinking he was some social media Lothario. He wasn't trying to impress her, but he definitely didn't want to turn her off. He was having too much fun. They ate their next several bites in amiable silence before setting aside the giant burgers and turning their attention to their fries.

Trick raised his hand to flag the waiter. "I'm going to need a beer with this. You?"

"Oh, I'd love a cocktail."

She'd surprised him again. He'd expected her to stick with water. "Then a cocktail you shall have."

He ordered a beer, and she ordered a peach Bellini. Trick shelved his many questions until their drinks arrived. Rylee lifted her peach fizzy drink to her lips and sipped. She emitted a delicate hum rather than a ravenous groan this time around, and he honestly didn't know which sound he preferred.

"One rarely finds a peach Bellini outside of brunch."

She took another swallow and nodded her agreement. "Don't I know it. I'm usually working on Saturday and Sunday mornings. I don't often see my favorite weekend meal. Ah, brunch." She'd said it so wistfully he had to smile. She lifted a fry and smiled back at him. Her lips were full, the shimmer of gloss still clinging to the edges of her mouth.

"So, let me get this straight. You hate your shoes, drink brunch drinks in the evening, and even though you're trying not to, you find me disturbingly attractive."

Her light skin slowly gained color, the pink tinge starting at her collarbone and creeping up her neck. She didn't falter, volleying back at him with a, "You're half right. I do find you disturbing."

He couldn't help laughing at her quick wit. She appeared pleased with herself as she lifted her burger and took another hearty bite.

"It's cool that you agreed to donating the money for your views for this event, though," she conceded a moment later. "I thought I'd have to fight you on that point."

"What I do isn't about the money."

She pursed her lips, her gaze softening. She was curious to know more, but he could feel her holding back. He had the idea that she held back often. In life. With other people. He was curious to know more about that as well. Maybe they'd spend more time together in the coming days and he could pry a few answers out of her.

"I may seem like a prankster who has nothing better to do than wedge my way into the spotlight, but that's the public's perception, not reality. You've worked with celebrity clients before, I assume?"

"Many."

"You know there are two sides to us. The public side and the private side."

"Isn't that true of everyone? I am wearing shoes I hate."

"You have a point."

She polished off the peach Bellini and then dug into her purse for her wallet.

"I've got it." He brandished a black metal credit card. "Don't argue with me, either."

She showed empty hands to him. "If you insist. Thank you."

"You're welcome."

"I should give you my number." She reached for her cellphone.

His heart galloped. Hell yes, she should. He hadn't been expecting them to hit it off at this dinner, but there was no doubt they had both enjoyed the company. He looked forward to seeing her again. More of her. A *lot* more of her.

"We are in agreement." He rattled off his phone number and his cellphone chimed a second later. Her incoming text read Hi.

She dropped her phone into her purse and stood. "You're going to need to reach me before you try to set foot in the Texas Cattleman's Club. Security is on alert to look out for riffraff."

Riffraff. He swallowed a chuckle. The word was tame enough to make him wonder if she had given him her number under the guise of business, when in actuality she'd wanted him to have it for pleasurable reasons.

"I'll be leaving for the TCC at 6 a.m. sharp tomorrow morning. I should go to bed."

"I'll see you there." Brighter and earlier than he'd intended, but he was already looking forward to going another round with her.

Three

Rylee's morning started at 5 a.m. She drank a coffee while she readied herself for the day. She chose a mauve dress with ruching on one side, where a tie fashioned into a loose bow hung. She paired the neutral garment with a pair of nude heels—no straps. Her hair was in its usual updo, pinned to resist the Texas winds should they kick up today.

An hour later—she had promised 6 a.m. sharp—she stepped out of the elevator to find Trick walking out of another elevator directly across from hers. They met in the middle, leaving about a foot of space between them. His gray trousers and short-sleeved pale blue crew-neck shirt managed to look dressy rather than casual. The color offset his dark hair and stubble nicely. He gave her a lazy blink, but didn't bother to conceal his surprise.

"Rylee." Hazel eyes perused her outfit before he gave her a grin. "You are stunning. Beautiful."

Unused to being complimented so thoroughly, she was suddenly bashful. She'd made it a habit to dress so that she blended into the background. The bride and groom were the stars. She was simply the woman behind the curtain.

"Let me." He adjusted the camera bag on his shoulder and reached for her tote. She relinquished the weighty bag, filled with everything she would need for the day—and more. He wrapped one fist around the straps and gave her an *I'm impressed* eyebrow lift when he tested its heft. "You didn't have to track me down at the hotel. I called a car."

"I'm staying in this hotel."

"You're staying *here*? I thought you lived in Royal."

"I grew up in Texas. I moved to LA after I started my business."

"You live in LA." *Like me*, his tone implied.

"Yes. My parents live in Royal. I've been staying with them since March, overseeing every detail of the wedding. The week of the wedding I like to be near the venue. I can't risk being unavailable because of traffic or weather or an unexpected incident."

"Like a blackout."

She tilted her head. "Or a wedding crasher."

His tired smile faded into a yawn, one he was unable to conceal since his hands were full. "Sorry. I'm never up this early. I'm exhausted."

"You get used to it."

They stepped outside into a wall of warmth. Even this early, Mother Nature had cranked up the heat. A car rolled to a stop at the curb.

"That's me. Want to carpool?"

"Uh…" She thought about what he'd said last night about them being partners. About how odd it'd sounded after months of viewing him as an adversary.

"Don't you want to reduce your carbon footprint?" Trick handed his own bag to the driver and held Rylee's bag in limbo while waiting for her answer.

"Sure. Why not?" No sense in driving separately when they were heading to the same place. He stowed her bag with his and then opened the door for her. She slid into the back seat, and he rounded the car and slid in next to her. The tight confines of their ride put them in close proximity again, and sooner than she'd expected. She inhaled the spicy notes of his cologne, her head spinning. Why did he have to look *and* smell so good?

Once the driver deposited them at the side entrance of the Texas Cattleman's Club and they had their bags, Rylee used her keycard to let herself into the private office she'd arranged for the week.

"Command central," Trick commented as they stepped inside.

She was already unpacking her laptop and a large binder onto the desk, preparing for the many possibilities the day would bring. "You're welcome to leave any equipment you don't need in here. I'm the only one with a key to this room, so your belongings will be safe."

He took a video camera and a handheld tripod with a rubber grip from his bag and then slid his cellphone into his pocket. “I’m all set. Where to first?”

“Wherever you’d like.” She waved him off, wary at the idea of him following her. “I’m going to be buzzing around.”

“Consider me your shadow. I have nowhere else to be.”

They started at the location of the ceremony, an open grassy area with a view of the mountains in the distance. The chairs, flowers and the arch wouldn’t arrive until the morning of, but she liked to have a feel for what to expect. As she walked, she pecked notes into her phone. Number one on her to-do list was to contact the groundskeeper to make sure they had mowing on their schedule for Friday.

As she walked, she kicked a crushed soda can. She picked it up, along with a piece of plastic wrapping that had come from who knew what. She *tsked.* This wouldn’t do at all.

“You pick up litter too? Full-service wedding planner.”

She turned to find him filming her. “What are you doing?”

"Documenting." He kept the camera pointing in her direction.

"Not *me*. The venue."

"You said I could record at my discretion. Besides, you're the planner, Rylee. Everything and everyone goes through you. You're the star of the pre-show." He lowered the camera and checked the footage. "How did I not notice your dimples yesterday?"

"I don't know. They're a bit much."

"I must've been dazzled." He glanced up from the camera screen. "I can't think when you smile."

She shook her head, still trying to weigh the Trick who, well, *tricked* everyone for views online, and the man she'd gone to dinner with who had been both polite and kind.

"There's no need to lay it on this thick," she said as she walked to a refuse bin. "I get it. You're charming, engaging. The life of the party."

"You think I'm buttering you up?"

"Aren't you?"

He seesawed his head as if he was considering. "I guess that depends. Is it working?"

She didn't deign him with an answer.

"Speaking of work, I have a lot of it to do. Stay out of any room marked private. The TCC has added extra security so you'll need this to walk around." She reached into her purse and pulled out a guest pass. "Everywhere else is open. I work better alone."

He accepted the pass and nodded. "Meet up with you in a few hours?"

"Text me if you can't find me."

He lifted the camera, pointing it at her again. "I'll look for the dimples. Can't miss 'em now."

He walked off, and she admired his tight backside for a beat before recovering her professionalism. She had a job to do and not a single item on her itinerary read *be charmed by Trick MacArthur.*

The fans were blowing on high on the covered porch at the rear of the club. Rylee sat in a rocker, leaned her head back and shut her eyes. She had been outside in the heat for most of the morning, walking the property as she made phone calls. She'd double-checked that the Chiavari chairs for the ceremony had arrived, which was important as they couldn't ask the guests to sit in the grass. Gold chairs had been harder to track down than white, as were many of the items required to match with Xavier and Ariana's theme. The old Hollywood glamor theme had been augmented, as had many other details over the last few months, to incorporate the state flower, the blue bonnet. A rich blue-purple shade had been added to the gold, black and cream color scheme.

Rylee had also called to the officiant to quadruple-check he'd be on time and that he'd received his payment. His assistant assured her that he'd arrive ready for the midmorning ceremony. An outdoor venue in Texas in June required an early ceremony, or else the guests would melt. Kind of like she was doing right now.

"There you are. I was about to give up." Trick stepped onto the porch from inside the club, a plastic bag in one hand and a pair of crystal flutes in the other. "This place is enormous." His tripod was tucked under his arm. He carefully set it aside as he placed the bag onto a side table next to her. He handed her a flute. "Peach Bellini."

She accepted the sweating glass, her mouth watering. “Seriously?”

“I figured one wouldn’t hurt.” He set his own glass down and extracted a Styrofoam container from the plastic bag. He cracked the lid and showed her the contents. “Crab and avocado eggs Benedict. The other box is full of pancakes.”

“You brought me brunch?” She was touched. Had anyone *ever* delivered her brunch?

She hadn’t had much male attention since she’d split up with Louis—the other reason for her fleeing Texas to live in LA—and that’d been over two years ago. She knew she should resist Trick’s advances, but a bigger part of her said *go for it*. It was just brunch. What was the harm? Then she heard herself resist anyway.

“This is so nice, but—”

“C’mon, Peaches. I brought you your favorite drink and the meal you are typically unable to enjoy before nine o’clock at night. Indulge.”

Well. Who could say no to that? Besides, she *was* thirsty.

She took a dainty sip of her drink, the bubbles tickling her throat. It was sweet and delicious and perfect. Trick pulled his shoulders back like he was proud of himself. He should be. No one had successfully wooed her away from her self-enforced work rules.

"That's more like it." He unrolled a set of silverware, sliced off a bite of the eggs Benedict, and offered it to her. She accepted the fork and fed herself, aware of him watching her closely.

"This is good."

"I'm glad you approve." He carved off another bite for her.

"Peaches, huh? Are you married to that nickname?"

"What an appropriate choice of words. And yes." He nodded. "I'm afraid it's going to stick. From the hue of your cheeks to the choice of your drinks. Peaches."

He was too much. Kind of like brunch and a Bellini at ten o'clock on a work day.

Trick opened the other box. The tantalizing smell of fresh pancakes wafted into the air. He poured maple syrup from the packet as Rylee moaned around her breakfast. He liked the sounds she made when she ate. It was the dominating reason he'd bought her brunch in the first place. Plus, it was nice to see her take a minute to enjoy something she clearly loved. He'd bet she didn't do that often enough. Meanwhile, he'd made a lifestyle out of it.

"How long have you been planning weddings?" He offered her a bite of pancake, dripping with sweet, sticky syrup. She reached for the fork, but he shook his head. "Better let me do it. This syrup has a mind of its own."

She admonished him with a look, but opened her mouth and allowed him to feed her. When a drop of maple syrup lingered at the corner of her mouth, he wiped it away with his thumb. His gaze locked with hers, he sucked the sugar off his thumb. Her blue eyes were unerring in their target—his mouth had piqued her interest.

He hadn't come to Texas to seduce Rylee. Or any woman, for that matter. But the more he'd watched her from afar, the more intrigued he'd become. She was stubborn and strong, poised and confident. He'd begun to wonder if she ever undid that knot from her hair, or wore a pair of short, frayed denim shorts. Last night when she'd left him sitting at the steakhouse alone, he'd wondered what she wore to bed. Then this morning he'd found out that she was staying in the same damn hotel he was staying in.

Intrigued didn't begin to describe how he felt whenever he was with her. He wanted to know more about her. He wanted to experience more *of* her. With the wedding a few days away, he was aware he was running out of time to impress her. Hence, the brunch delivery.

She gathered the perfect bite of avocado and crab, egg and English muffin and offered it to him. He took the fork as she answered his earlier question.

"Almost three years." Her eyebrows knit. "Has it already been three years? It simultaneously feels like I've been doing this forever and like I just started."

"Time's funny like that. I feel like I've been doing what I do for so long I should be eighty years old by now."

"How long have you been a social media influencer?"

His mouth screwed to the side. He didn't care for that title. "I didn't set out to influence anyone. I wanted to entertain them. My focus has changed in the last year."

"How so?" She leaned in the slightest bit, her rocker inching forward. Her pretty blue eyes settled on him, giving off serious all-American girl vibes.

Until today he would have claimed not to have a type, but this curvy blonde was currently occupying the number one spot at the top of that list. He'd never wanted to film someone so badly in his life, but he didn't want to lose the momentum of their friendly conversation.

"I'm serving up what the world needs most," he answered. "Joy can be in short supply when something scary is happening. Lately the world is full of scary shit."

"No kidding." Her eyebrows bent, suggesting that her world was more than hearts and roses. At first blush, she came off like a perfectionist romantic. But he knew people. Everyone had hidden layers—she was no exception.

"We deserve to laugh. Deserve to be happy.

And it's far simpler than most people think. Look how happy you are right now, Peaches. Takeout and a Bellini. Simple."

Her dimples indented her cheeks when she smiled. He still had no idea how in the hell he'd overlooked those. He leaned in, eager to hear what she would say next. Had she changed her mind about him? Or did she still view him as the bad boy with the bad reputation?

"Nothing is ever simple," she said, answering the question in his head.

Four

What was Trick's angle? Rylee couldn't figure him out. Obviously, it was wise for him to stay on her good side. She had given him the offer of a lifetime, after all. Which reminded her, she needed to let Xavier and Ariana know about this arrangement. Ari had been worried about Trick's antics, and Rylee had managed to come up with a palatable solution. It wasn't like her to ask for forgiveness rather than permission, but she had run out of time.

He lifted his own Bellini and took a sip. "Damn. That is good."

"Well, yeah." She polished off the rest of

her glass, already feeling better. She would call Ari today and straighten this out. No worries.

"Have you always been detail-oriented? Not much slides by you," he said.

"Are you referring to yourself?"

His boyish, wicked grin was utterly charming. She'd bet he could've gone everywhere he pleased inside the Texas Cattleman's Club, pass or no.

"Not always," she told him. "Not until I found myself planning a wedding."

Her own wedding, to be precise, but it was way too early for that conversation. If she were two Bellinis in, maybe.

"I have trouble focusing. ADHD." He pointed to himself, seemingly unashamed to admit it. Not that he should be, but Louis hadn't liked admitting to his flaws. "Thank goodness for short-form videos trending right now or I'd be up to my eyeballs in editing."

"You don't edit the videos yourself?"

"That's a job for my editing team."

"You have an editing *team*?" She had assumed Trick was running a one-man show; filming, editing and posting on his own.

"Hell yes. And a few people who do nothing but research hashtags and reply to comments on my behalf. There are a lot of moving parts in the life of a wedding crasher." He leaned back on the rocker, his elbow propped on the arm, looking casual and, okay, she'd admit it. *Fun.*

For all the fun Rylee planned, she hadn't reserved much for herself. Which was probably what rankled her most about Trick. He had fun constantly, and at the expense of everyone who'd worked hard to plan the events he crashed. "Do you ever feel badly for showing up to drink the drinks and eat the food and party with the guests at an event where you contributed nothing?"

His eyebrows lifted.

She didn't blink. It was a fair question.

"You don't think I contribute?"

She held up her cellphone. "When was the last time you called vendors to ensure there are enough chairs for the ceremony? Have you ever made a last-minute trip to the dollar store in search of votive cups? What about a champagne shortage, which required you to phone a friend and ask if they have a spare bottle or two tucked away for a special occasion?"

He didn't take offense to her line of questioning, and neither did he sit up straight. He stayed in that same lounging position, taking care to finish his drink before answering. "Have *you* ever started a conga line at a wedding reception to liven up a stale dance floor? Or fast-danced with a four-year-old flower girl when her family was too tired to indulge her? How many times have you threatened a guest with bodily harm when he is sniffing around the gift table looking for envelopes filled with cash?" He set his glass on the table and dropped his elbows to his knees, peering up at her with such earnestness that she squirmed in her seat.

She hadn't done any of those things, which he must have assumed.

"Do you enjoy the receptions of the weddings you plan? Or are you on the clock until the last guest leaves?"

"There is always the possibility something could go wrong." She elevated her chin defensively.

"True. But who said *you* have to prevent every possible accident?"

"And who put *you* in charge of being the life of the party and/or temporary security guard?"

He sat back and pulled in a deep breath. "So, we agree. We've assigned ourselves our roles."

"At least I'm invited to the events."

"And paid. I shell out a lot of money to be there."

She assumed he was referring to the cost of traveling to the event, or buying a new suit. Camera equipment was expensive.

"As far as invitations," he continued, "those come later for me. Baby showers. Birthday parties. One second wedding for a groom."

"You keep in touch with them?" That surprised her.

"I don't seek it, but some of them reach out. It's not uncommon for the bride and groom to thank me for being there, or send me photos that I'm in."

She had to laugh. *What in the Owen Wilson...?* Was Trick serious?

"So because of your history," she said, "you

thought you'd win over Ari and Ex the same way? By crashing their high-profile wedding and, what, *wooing* grandmothers or bridesmaids, or, or…"

"Wedding planners?"

She pursed her lips.

"I didn't plan on *wooing* anyone. Just like I didn't plan on becoming a professional wedding crasher. I happen to excel at it, so that's what I do."

"Are you talking about the wooing or the crashing?"

"You tell me." He let that comment dangle. "I fell into this business, but I don't regret it."

Rylee had fallen into her career as well. It was odd learning all that they had in common. She'd relegated Trick to *The Enemy* and frankly, was more comfortable with that dynamic than the idea of them on the same side.

"I should go to the office. I have a handful of emails to return I've been putting off." She reached down and massaged her heel. At least she'd be sitting behind a desk for a few hours and could stop walking around in these stupid shoes.

"They have a spa in our hotel. You should book a massage and a foot soak. You deserve it, considering the hell you put your feet through."

"I paid a lot of money for these shoes." She stood, wincing as one of those very expensive shoes pinched her pinky toe.

"You're worth the pampering, Peaches. Want me to schedule it for you?"

"No." But she spoke the word around a small smile. What was it with this guy? Did he cast a spell on everyone he met? She'd been determined to dislike him before they'd struck this bargain and was losing that battle gradually. *One Bellini at a time.*

He gathered up their trash and the flutes and followed her inside.

"Are you coming to the office with me?"

"Only temporarily. I have a drone to unpack."

She stopped short of unlocking the door. "You have a drone?"

"Yeah. For overhead shots. It's fun. You want to drive?"

"No."

"You are way too comfortable with that word, Peaches. When's the last time you said yes?"

Door open, she turned to face him. He was close, within kissing distance if one was considering kissing him…which she was *not.* She propped a hand on the doorknob effectively blocking his path into the office.

"Mr. MacArthur, the most effective way to persuade me to say yes would be if you asked if you can leave early, stay out of the way, or be a no-show to the wedding and reception."

He shook his head slowly. "You're wrong about that, Ms. Meadows. The most effective way to persuade you to say yes is to stay in your space as much as possible. You've already said yes to dinner, yes to sharing a car, and yes to brunch."

She had. She didn't like the reminder that she was losing her willpower where he was concerned. "Only because you said yes to me first."

"Know what else?" he continued as if she hadn't spoken. "I don't think you mind me in your space. I think you might *like* me in your space. I think—"

She lifted her hand and pressed her fingertips against his lips. Her heart raced at the touch, more intimate than she'd anticipated. His lips flinched into a half-smile.

"Are you through?" she whispered.

"Nope." He moved her hand aside. "Just getting started."

Ariana Ramos had a great laugh. It was nearly impossible not to join in, or at least smile with her. Especially over video call, which was how Rylee had reached out. "Rye, this is why I pay you. I trust you."

Rylee released the tension from her shoulders, relieved to have finally confessed about the arrangement with Trick. "I'm glad to hear that you aren't upset. I sort of proceeded without you."

Ari had stayed resolutely silent while Rylee had explained the situation, and when Ari's facial expression remained neutral, Rylee had felt the need to explain *more*. When she'd finally stopped explaining, Ari fingered her short hair and let out another laugh that lifted her cheeks.

"I'll be honest with you, I was paranoid

for a while that he was going to swoop in and ruin everything. Now that I know you have him under control, I am almost excited to meet this man." Ari lowered herself onto a tuffet in what Rylee recognized as Natalie Valentine's bridal shop.

Rylee wouldn't say that she had Trick "under control" but she wasn't going to volunteer that information.

"He's won over my unflappable wedding planner? Unheard of!"

Since Rylee and Ariana had become friends over the course of planning this wedding, Rylee knew to take that as a compliment. She kept her polite smile, but an old wound that lived within her had opened up at the mention of the word "unflappable." It inferred a rigidity that Louis had pointed out often in their relationship. In a way, Trick had pointed that out as well.

"It's less about winning me, or you and Xavier, over and more about him agreeing to behave and share only the footage of the wedding plans rather than the wedding itself."

"I trust you implicitly." Ari adjusted the bodice of a black dress adorned with bright pink and purple flower embroidery. “You’ve rolled with a blackout, vendor issues, *and* a wedding crasher and you didn’t flinch.”

Oh, Rylee had flinched plenty, but she was more of a crying-on-the-inside kind of girl. She’d had her minor meltdown moments over the last few months, but hopefully she’d concealed the majority of her true feelings. As much as she treasured both Ariana and Xavier, this wedding had been the most trying in her professional experience.

“You’re the priority, Ari. Ex is *just* the groom.”

Ari’s chiming laughter rang out again.

“I can see that you’re at the bridal shop. How did the final fitting go?”

“Wonderful!” The future bride’s face lit up, her wide, pink-lipped smile causing her brown eyes to crinkle at the edges. “Keely is a true artist. And she integrated blue bonnets into the design in a subtle, beautiful way.”

“She’s amazing. I’m not surprised.” Even though they weren’t from the same part of the country, Rylee could relate to the born-and-raised-in-New-York designer. Keely had been focused on each and every detail of the dress, and not only because she knew that photographs of Ari in it would boost her career in a big way. Keely cared about details because she was committed to excellence.

Rylee wrinkled her nose. She wished she would have mentioned to Trick that excellence was the reason she appeared rigid. If that's what he thought of her. He seemed to delight in talking her into doing things she shouldn't be doing while on the clock. Like drinking Bellinis.

"I have to run, but keep me posted on the gift bags, okay?" Ari had her own lifestyle brand and had been selective about the gifts for each and every guest to take home. "Look for a gift from me to you, too. It should arrive this evening."

"You didn't have to do that," Rylee said, meaning it. Ari had already been so generous.

"Rye, I didn't do it because I had to. I did it because we're friends. I recognize a hardworking woman who doesn't take enough time for herself when I see one." Ari gave the screen an air kiss. "See you soon, doll."

"Definitely," Rylee said around a lump in

her throat. She ended the video call. She had known she and Ari were friendly, but hearing the other woman verify that they were "friends" had touched her. Also, Ari gave great gifts. Rylee was looking forward to opening the care package as soon as it arrived.

Five

Rylee, sitting at the desk in her private office at the TCC, heard her cellphone ping and regarded it with one eye open. She was afraid of what else might potentially go wrong now that they were within spitting distance of the wedding.

So far she'd been contacted about a transportation issue with the vintage cars the best man had lined up for wedding, as well as the fact that some of the accessories for the reception had been shipped to the wrong address. Thankfully, that address belonged to a nearby hotel where Ariana's sister, Sasha Ramos, was staying. Rylee had arranged for a courier to pick up the boxes from Sasha and bring them to the TCC.

She needed to ensure the packages arrived safely and were stored in the correct ballroom, as well as follow up with Tripp about the car situation. A wedding planner's work was truly never done.

Then the call had come from Keely, who was hand-delivering the wedding gown to Rylee at Ari's request. They'd agreed to conceal it in a black dress bag and for it to be locked in Rylee's temporary private office here at the TCC. Rylee couldn't very well stash it in her hotel room, in case there was a sneaky paparazzo who paid off a member of the hotel staff to snap a pic or two. Ironically, she trusted Trick more than a random photographer.

Speaking of, the text message on her phone's screen was from Trick. He hadn't contacted her with an emergency, but a request: Lunch?

"All he does is eat." Was it noon already? She checked the clock on the wall. It read ten after three. "*Three?* It's three o'clock?"

"My point exactly." Trick entered through her open office door holding a charcuterie plate overflowing with cheeses, various meats, plump green grapes, nuts and honeycomb.

"Do I want to know where you stole that from?"

"I did not steal it. I requested it from the kitchen. Pamela is really nice."

Rylee didn't know Pamela, but the idea of him charming charcuterie out of another woman was an unpleasant thought.

"These, though"—from behind his back, he brandished two cans of Perrier—"I stole off a cart by the bar."

"Are you serious?"

"No. God. What do you take me for? Ricardo was restocking, and I asked if I could buy a few cans. He wouldn't let me pay, but I did ask."

She didn't know Ricardo either. How was it that Trick was already on a first-name basis with people at an exclusive club he didn't belong at or belong to? Incredible.

He set down the tray of finger foods and she didn't hesitate. She stacked a chunk of Gouda on top of a Genoa salami slice and ate it. She'd had no idea how hungry she was until that first bite. He cracked open a can of Perrier and set it in front of her.

"I considered bringing you chardonnay, but I didn't want to push the boundaries of your work rules. Especially since you're finishing up for the day."

The water was lime-flavored and refreshing. "I'm far from finishing up. The dress designer is delivering Ari's dress, and I need to call Tripp about the vintage cars. Plus, there is a courier on the way with some items for the reception hall. I need to check the deliveries that were already stacked in that room and ensure they are for Ari and Ex and not like, a box of toilet paper rolls meant for maintenance instead."

Trick laughed, sobering when she didn't laugh with him. "Wait. For real? That has happened before?"

"Yes. Maintenance received the candles for the candelabras and left them in the warehouse on a day when it was 105 degrees outside."

He winced.

"That's something I'll never allow to happen again." One of many mistakes she'd learned from since starting this business.

"I've been to a lot of weddings, and I've met a handful of wedding planners, but I never bothered finding out what was involved. Much more than I thought."

"Were you too busy trying to take off their shoes or their skirts?" It wasn't hard to imagine Trick with a besotted woman dangling off his arm.

"I was avoiding them. They didn't approach me with an offer like you did. I knew that they would spot me from a mile away. Being friendly with the planner would make it harder to blend in. That's why I crash weddings in the middle and not at the start. After everyone has eaten and downed a few drinks."

"So this is a whole new adventure for you."

"Completely." He ate a cracker topped with prosciutto. "So, do you want me to hang out here and wait for Keely or head to the reception hall to meet the courier?"

Rylee blinked, surprised by the offer. She'd relegated herself to doing everything. "I've got it."

He unpacked a tripod from his bag. "I want to shoot some footage of the reception hall anyway. I'm going to film the progress each day and then show a big reveal of the end result."

"In a time-lapse?" she guessed.

"Maybe. I haven't decided how to handle the footage yet. But people are begging for a livestream, so maybe I'll pop open some of the boxes with you and we'll find out if we have candles or Cottonelle."

She laughed.

"So? Reception hall?" He pointed one thumb over his shoulder and waited for her answer. Part of her wanted to argue that it wasn't his responsibility to meet the courier, but she couldn't be two places at once. She didn't want to miss Keely.

"Sure."

He dipped his head in a nod. Before he was out the door, she called out her thanks. He didn't turn around when he answered, "No problem, Peaches."

On his way to the reception area, Trick encountered the courier. The girl was around his younger sister's age, twenty or so, and wearing boots and a uniform of shorts and a shirt with her name stitched above the left pocket. She looked worried, and he'd bet a hundred bucks that her quivering chin would lead to tears if someone didn't intervene.

The big brother in him went on high alert. He angled toward her, intercepting her as she checked the clipboard in her hands for the third time.

"Mackenzie. Are you the courier I'm searching for?" He gave her a smile to set her at ease.

"Y-yes. Are you Rylee?" There was a hint of doubt in her voice as she looked him up and down.

"Rylee sent me. I'm Patrick." He grinned. "I'm happy to help carry the boxes if that's the issue. The reception hall is right around the corner." As he spoke, he watched the girl's face go slack and mouth drop open.

"Oh, my god. You're—you're Trick MacArthur. The wedding crasher. Oh, my god!"

"Ah, yeah." He sent a nervous look around the empty corridor. "I'm here on official business though, no crashing."

"You have a camera." The girl's smile was

unstoppable, her earlier turmoil forgotten. "What are you filming?"

"It's a surprise."

"Can I have a photo of you? Please?"

"Sure." He acquiesced, leaning in and smiling as she took a selfie of them and checked the screen of her phone.

"Thank you! Thank you. Wow. Trick MacArthur." Then her face fell as her earlier worries flooded in and washed away her smile. "Shit. I mean, shoot. I'm, uh, I have a problem."

"Need a dolly for the delivery? Is it too heavy to carry?"

She gave him a dubious look. "Not at all. I left the box in the car until I found out where I was going. I can carry it. But I'm running late for my next delivery."

"Oh-kay." He was lost. If she was in a hurry, why was she standing here talking to him instead of sprinting back to her car? "How about I bring the box in myself, and then you can leave for your next delivery."

"I can't ask you to do that." Awe slipped into her gaze before she frowned. "I can't leave for my next delivery. I have a flat tire."

There was the chin quiver again. "I cancelled triple-A because I never used it, and I'm new at this stupid job and now I'm going to be fired."

Ah-ha. Now he was caught up. "We won't let that happen, Mackenzie. First off, I can change a tire. And secondly, you have a cell-phone. Film me changing the tire and you will have proof to show your boss that you weren't lying about the delay."

"Really?" He knew a look of hero worship when he saw it. The one Mackenzie wore now was reminiscent of the way his sister, Cassie, looked at him when he'd picked her up from a party at 2 a.m. and didn't tell their parents she'd sneaked out.

"Lead the way." He held out an arm and the courier bounced toward the exit, checking over her shoulder on the way like she was making sure he hadn't vanished into thin air.

Walking outside was like walking into one of the circles of hell. The heat was stifling, taking his breath and causing sweat to bead above his upper lip. If Texas heat was hell, then air-conditioning must be heaven.

Heaven, kind of like Rylee's pale pink lip

gloss and dimples whenever she smiled at him. She'd smiled at him when he brought her lunch today. He was already trying to think of more ways to beckon those dimples forth.

"This is me," Mackenzie gestured to the hatchback parked on the curb.

It'd been a while since he had changed a tire. He silently hoped it was like riding a bike. The box destined for Ariana and Xavier's reception area was awkwardly shaped but weighed next to nothing. He helped unpack the shipment beneath it next. The boxes were considerably heavy by his definition and yet the young female courier lifted them without issue.

Once the boxes were out of the way, and he had the donut spare tire and jack in hand, he ratcheted up the car and got to work.

"I had a bit of trouble at the job today," Mackenzie was saying. "And you will never believe who I ran into. A knight in wedding-crashing armor!"

He recognized the cadence of someone narrating a video. No stranger to being on camera, he raised a hand to wave before returning his attention to the tire.

"Trick MacArthur is at the Texas Cattleman's Club!" Mackenzie whisper-screamed as she videoed herself. "What are the odds? I'm literally *dead*!"

He had to smile, even while sweating his ass off and simultaneously ruining his favorite shirt with a grease stain. And while trying to remember how to loosen and tighten a lug nut so that Mackenzie didn't suffer a fiery car crash on the way to her next delivery.

Her being starstruck over their chance encounter had done more than boost his ego. It had reminded him the reason behind everything he did. The *people.*

He'd always been about more than clicks, follows or beating the pesky algorithm. Sure, he'd been guilty of being caught up in the numbers in the past, but he'd grown up a lot since then.

Mackenzie, still filming and likely assuming he couldn't hear her, whispered loudly into her phone's speaker. "Isn't he hot?"

Six

"Thanks so much, Keely." Rylee accepted the hug from the dress designer, who was taller than her and then some with the added help of three-inch pumps.

"You know I have to see this all the way through." The other woman's smile could light an entire room, but the way she held herself kept anyone from thinking she was only here for the party. Keely was fastidious about her work, which Rylee related to, and respected.

"I'll be seeing you at the wedding, I assume?" Rylee knew that Keely was romantically linked to Jay Chatman, a close friend of the groom.

"Yes," Keely lifted a finger to smooth her eyebrow. "We will be there. I'll also be in Royal a lot more. I have my own space at Jay's, so I'll be working in Texas whenever I can."

A man in a cowboy hat opened the side door and held it for them. Keely's flowy sleeves blew in the warm breeze that swirled around them as they exited.

"I'm sure our paths will cross again. You're at the top of my list for a designer whenever a bride needs a recommendation. If you are able to carve out time in your soon-to-be exploding schedule and in between jet-setting across the globe as a famous designer."

"Stop." Keely gave Rylee's arm a playful tap. "I'll be jet-setting, but I'll always make time for the people I care about. You're one of the good ones, Rylee Meadows."

Rylee was warmed by the compliment. She thought of Keely as a friend, and liked hearing that the feeling was mutual.

"Hey, isn't that your wedding crasher?"

Rylee turned in the direction Keely pointed.

Trick was grinning for the camera and chatting with a young woman standing next to her car. By her uniform, Rylee assumed this was the courier she'd sent for. A small crowd had gathered, and Rylee quickly deduced why. Trick held a jack in one hand and there was a grease stain on his shirt.

"He's not technically *mine*," she grumbled.

"I'll let you tend to that…situation." Keely let out a chuckle. "He is cute, though."

Cute? Trick was far from "cute." With his powerful forearm muscles on display, his dark, wavy hair blowing in the hot Texas air and the grin on his face, he was nothing short of gorgeous.

As if drawn in by his sheer magnetism, Rylee approached the car where a handful of people had gathered. Because Trick had put on a show and changed a tire, or because they'd recognized him?

The latter, she soon gathered. The girl wasn't snapping photos, she was filming. He took his eyes off the girl's front-facing camera screen when he saw Rylee coming their way.

"There she is." His grin seemed more real for her. "Mackenzie, this is Rylee Meadows."

The camera swung around to face Rylee and her steps faltered.

"She's pretty," Mackenzie said. "Your girlfriend?"

Trick took the question in stride, but his answer shocked Rylee all the way down to her uncomfortable shoes. "Not yet."

Mackenzie ended the video after promising her audience she would post more later, and then she pocketed her phone. "Ms. Meadows. Can you sign for this?" She handed off a clipboard that had been tucked under her arm. "I brought the package you requested."

Trick hefted a sizable box, showing her. "Weighs next to nothing."

"No, it shouldn't." Rylee scribbled her name on the form.

"I was running late because of a flat tire. Trick saved me." The younger woman's face glowed with admiration as she turned to face him. "Thanks again. I'll see you online?"

"You sure will."

With a delighted little squeal, Mackenzie climbed into her car, waved goodbye and drove out of the club's driveway.

"I couldn't say no," Trick explained as he

adjusted the large box in his arms. "She was almost in tears. Reminded me so much of my younger sister, Cassie, my heart broke a little."

That was sweet, actually.

"She recognized me." He elbowed the accessibility button to open the automatic door for the side entrance. "Didn't expect that."

"I noticed you let her film you." At the reception hall, Rylee extracted her keycard and opened the door for him. "Are you always so magnanimous?"

"Nothing new about being on camera for me." He stepped into the darkened room. Rylee flipped on the lights. The venue wasn't much to look at in the moment, but come Saturday, this room would be transformed into old Hollywood utopia. Right now there were boxes upon boxes, several long tables set up in rows and a fully stocked bar in the corner. "Whoa."

"Not what you expected?" she asked as he set the large box onto one of the naked tables.

"I'm not used to seeing this stage. My followers are always begging me for behind-the-scenes stuff. They're going to love this, and it's all thanks to you." He set up his tripod and then ran back and forth from light switches to screen in search the perfect lighting.

Rylee was double-checking the other boxes to ensure that they did, in fact, belong here, when one of the sconces in the center of the room flickered and buzzed.

That was no good.

"I'll be right back," she called out. Trick gave her the thumbs-up signal. Before she left the room she couldn't help adding, "And then we'll talk about that not-yet comment."

He'd wondered if she was going to mention that. Now he knew. Rylee Meadows was not a woman who would take a comment about her being his girlfriend in stride. Even if she thought he'd said it simply for the public. Which he had, but that didn't mean there wasn't a nugget of truth to it.

He intended to win her over in the days ahead. By his estimations, and by the way she was checking him out a minute ago, he was closer to kissing those lips than before.

Once he had the lighting right, he swapped

the camera out for his cellphone and fired up a live video. He typed the title into the keyboard, which read *Early peek at the Noble-Ramos wedding in Royal!* And then hit the record button.

Talking to the camera came naturally to him, so when he addressed his invisible audience, he did so with ease. No longer did he have to practice what he was going to say in the mirror five times before he started. No longer did he suffer heart palpitations before tapping the big red button.

He moved the tripod to the bar and positioned himself behind it. Both hands on the bar top, he announced, "And this is where Ariana and Xavier's guests will be served, among other libations, the signature cocktail for their wedding. If you want to know what it is, you'll have to stick around for my interview with them on Friday night."

He glanced up when Rylee reentered the room, and then did a second take. She was hauling a ladder and a plastic bag. Not a stepladder, either. A full, six-foot-tall *ladder* ladder. She was about a mile away from him, so

Trick thought fast, grabbed the tripod and continued the tour while moving closer to her.

"Tables are set up but not decked out," he narrated. "The chairs, stacked against the walls." He panned over to the chairs lining one wall and sent Rylee a glare communicating that she could have—*should* have—asked for his help with the ladder. It looked heavy, and she was hardly dressed for manual labor.

"All of these boxes are filled with accessories, including this one…" He stopped where he'd set the box on the table and drummed his fingers on the top. Then he rested the tripod on the ground and angled the camera on his phone at Rylee who was currently climbing the ladder in front of him. Facing the camera, he mugged for his audience—1,890 watching, not bad—and then he said in a low voice, "Now if you'll excuse me, I'm going to aid the wedding planner with this highly dangerous task she's attempting to complete without my help." He turned away before quickly turning back to say, "I know this is the age of equal rights and she is capable of doing anything she damn well pleases, but ladies, hear me." He paused for effect before continuing,

"Take advantage of the men who are struck stupid by your beauty. *Use us.* We'll do whatever you want."

With that, he turned and walked to the ladder, careful not to startle Rylee, who either hadn't noticed or didn't care what or whom he was filming. He reached out to steady the ladder at the same instant the heel of one of her shoes snapped clean off.

She let out a dainty "Ahh!" as she lost her balance. Then she practically sat on his chest. He held tight to the sides of the ladder as she jerked away from him. Wobbling slightly, her wide eyes snapped to his.

"You okay?"

"Of cour—ahh!" Another wobble set her off balance, and he reacted without thinking, letting go of the ladder to wrap his arms around her. They fell to the ground, him padding the blow and landing hard on his ass.

He let out an "oof", but a low groan followed. That was because each and every one of Rylee's soft, supple curves was pressed against him. She was splayed awkwardly over top of him, her hair coming loose from her updo, her blue eyes burning into his. When her mouth dropped open invitingly, he decided to RSVP with a kiss.

He lifted his head to bring his lips closer to hers, when he noticed her raised hand. A hand that was delicately gripping a…light bulb? Both their gazes rerouted to that single, unbroken bulb and then back to each other.

"What the hell are you doing?" she snapped.

"Breaking your fall."

"I could have broken *you*. I'm not a petite woman, you know."

"You're perfect." His hands were resting innocuously on her waist, one of his legs nestled between hers. Every inch of her that was touching him was divine.

She appeared more inconvenienced than embarrassed as she rolled off him and straightened the skirt of her dress. She took off the shoe with the broken heel, and that's when she noticed the camera. He watched as her expression slowly morphed from inconvenienced to pissed off.

He stood to explain, but she swiveled his body so that his head blocked the camera. Her whisper even sounded angry. "What the hell, Trick?"

"We're live. Let's play it up. For Ari and Ex's sake." He nodded subtly, not giving her a chance to react before he knelt and slipped her other shoe off. He felt her hand on his shoulder and then he stood to introduce her.

"Ladies and gentleman, the lovely Rylee making a grand entrance. She's the wedding planner, and apparently is owed a new pair of..."—he turned his head to the side to read the inner sole of the shoe in his hand—"Sergio Rossi pumps."

Rylee futzed with her dress, clearly trying to rein in her temper. "You shouldn't sneak up on a girl while she's doing her own dirty work."

"You should have asked for my help."

"I don't need your help." Her cheeks grew pink.

"I didn't say you *needed* it. I said you should have asked for it. Hasn't it become apparent that I am willing to chase you around with Bellinis and brunch or charcuterie boards? I can change a light bulb." He snatched the bulb from her hand and started for the ladder.

"It's the last one!" she said when he set one foot on the bottom rung. "Be careful."

He cradled the bulb in his hand, more carefully now that he knew it was a rare commodity. “Okay, okay.”

At the top of the ladder, that she was steadying, he noticed, he replaced the flickering bulb for the one in his hand. He came down without incident, but then he didn’t have spikes on the heels of his shoes.

Once he was safely on the ground, he waggled the dead bulb at the screen of his phone, coming close to sign off. Now there were—*holy shit*—4,732 viewers on the live video.

“How many wedding crashers does it take to screw in a light bulb?” he asked, but the comments moving up the screen didn’t attempt to answer his corny joke. Instead they were painting him as a hero, and Rylee as his “girlfriend.”

The last comment he read followed that word with several crying emoji faces. He tried not to laugh. Clearly, they were interested in what was happening between him and the wedding planner. Who was he to sign off when his fans were begging for more?

Seven

Rather than stop the video, Trick turned toward Rylee. With a wink and a smile to let her know he was going to be teasing her, he held up the bulb between the fingers of one hand. "Where did you get this? And the ladder?"

"The maintenance closet." She shifted on her bare feet, never breaking eye contact with him. He wasn't sure when, but he'd won her over to the idea of playing it up for the camera. She was willing, which made this *fun*.

"The maintenance closet." He set down the spent bulb and circled her like a detective on a TV show questioning a suspect. "And was there a maintenance person there when you were in this closet, Ms. Meadows?"

She pressed her lips together, he assumed to hide a laugh at his over-the-top theatrics, but maintained her serious facade. He would have guessed that she'd be annoyed with his antics by now, but for whatever reason—his mentioning Ari and Ex might have helped—she'd decided to play it up as he'd requested.

"There was no maintenance person available, Mr. MacArthur."

"Am I to believe that the staff at the highly acclaimed Texas Cattleman's Club leaves their maintenance closet unattended *and* unlocked?" he asked with a flourish.

She shot out her chin and said the very last thing he'd expected her to say. "I can pick a lock."

Trick dropped character to grin. His audience had to be going crazy for this content. How could they not? She was gorgeous and stubborn and had confessed to a minor B&E.

Hands propped on his hips, he sort of repeated, "You picked the lock?"

Apparently she wasn't the least bit sorry.

She doubled down, stating, "It comes in handy more often than you think."

"Remind me to call you if I need to plan a heist, Peaches. Lock-picking would come in handy for a jewelry store. Or a bank. You could do better than light bulbs." He swept a stray blond hair behind her ear, his eyes roaming over her face. She leaned her cheek into the hand he'd raised. Realizing he didn't have full control of his faculties and even less of his hammering heart, he blinked and stepped away from her to address the camera.

"You heard it here, folks. If a bank gets robbed in Royal…" He pointed at the beautiful amateur thief. "Rylee Meadows. More to come. *Crash you later.*" He tapped the red button to stop recording. The comments that scrolled by read, "*Go for it, Trick!* And *Kiss her, Trick!*" Not that he blamed his fans. Kissing Rylee had certainly crossed his mind. Which was why he'd stopped the live video.

"You called me Peaches in front of a million online viewers."

"Just under five thousand," he said. "I didn't even mean to say it. It's just—"

"Just what?" She cocked her head as he approached. When he was standing in front of her, slightly taller than she was since she'd lost the heels, he answered her.

"It's just that I've imagined kissing you at least a hundred times since you took that first sip of a peach Bellini at the steakhouse. Whenever I look at your lips, I wonder if they taste like peaches."

He realized, perhaps belatedly, that he was within slapping distance. Not only had he filmed her *and* outed her as a thief on a live social media feed, but now he'd admitted he wanted to kiss her. But Rylee didn't slap him.

Her expression took on an almost angelic quality, even as challenge straightened her shoulders. "Well? What are you waiting for?"

He slid his palm from her cheek to the back of her neck. "Not a single fucking thing."

He pressed his lips against hers, answering their prayers. Her mouth was plush and warm. *God*—perfect. She didn't taste like peaches, but she did taste like a woman he'd like to taste a hell of a lot more *of.*

His other arm locked around her back, he hugged her curvy body as he slid his tongue over hers. She stroked his back with her short nails, the friction causing a stir behind the fly of his pants.

Electricity skittered along his scalp and jettisoned down his spine. He was on fire for this woman, and over what? A single kiss? A kiss that came to an abrupt end when it became clear they were not alone.

"Are we…interrupting?" came an amused-sounding voice from behind them. Before he turned to look, he soaked up Rylee's dazed expression. Definitely, they were continuing this later.

He released her neck, but kept his other hand on her back to steady her—or himself. Hard to tell.

He didn't recognize the couple in the doorway, but as soon as the woman spoke he knew she recognized him.

"Rylee. Hi." The woman flipped her shoulder-length, sable-colored hair and addressed Trick next. "You must be the 'juvenile, fame-seeking prankster who crashes high-profile weddings.' I'm paraphrasing Rylee, but that is close, isn't it?"

"Um…" Rylee was at a loss for words, a

novel concept. He didn't take offense to the insult, but instead extended a hand to the other woman.

"Trick MacArthur."

"Dionna Reed." She gestured at the man who stood at her side. "This is Tripp Noble."

"Maid of honor, and best man, respectively," Rylee supplemented.

"Of course." Trick had heard Rylee mention their names before. "Nice to meet you, Dionna, Tripp."

"You can call me Dee. Apparently you are no longer the enemy." To Rylee, she said, "Ari told me about your agreement with Trick. And then she dispatched us to check on the 'state of affairs.' Her words."

"Our reporting back to Ari and Ex has no bounds." Tripp sounded less inconvenienced than amused. He surveyed the stacks of boxes in the room. "What are we missing?"

"Nothing now." Rylee rushed to the box that Trick had carried in. She unfolded the top to reveal…feathers? "The pens were delivered to Sasha's hotel by mistake, but here they are. And it looks like they're all here."

Trick extracted a chunky gold pedestal with

multiple holes in it and then lifted one of the feather-tipped pens. They were ornate, with gold nibs and bands, the black faux feathers full and silky. He set the pedestal upright on the table and stuck a pen in it. Rylee and Dee began helping. Once every pen was in place, the pedestal looked more like a vase with a waterfall of feathers sprouting out of it.

"For the guest book," Rylee explained.

"It's gorgeous," Dee said approvingly. "What a find!"

"Thank you. Of course I'll ensure each of the pens work and I'll find some backup pens that are attractive in case one of the decorative pens run out of ink."

Trick swallowed a smile. That was his Rylee, planning for every unlikely hiccup. While that trait was admirable, he suspected her over-attention to detail caused more problems in her life than it solved.

"Keely brought the dress by already. I have it locked safe and sound in my private office here in the TCC. You never know who could be lurking around."

"Yeah, I see that." Dee slid Trick a look, but to him it felt approving.

"Now that you're both here, how about drinks?" Trick offered. "I'm buying."

Dee exchanged glances with Tripp and then Rylee.

"I was actually going to call about the vintage car situation, anyway," Rylee said. "Drinks would give us a chance to chat."

"In that case"—Tripp extended an arm toward the exit—"Lead the way."

Rylee had worked with Dee closely over the last few months. Dee had been making decisions for the bride whenever Ari couldn't be here. Not to mention Tripp had practically mind-read Rylee's plans for an Old Hollywood glamor wedding theme.

They relocated to the Silver Saddle, a tapas bar within the Bellamy, the same hotel where Trick and Rylee were staying. The bar was luxurious yet comfortable. Tripp chose a stand-up table with four high stools, one of which he pulled out for Dee.

"I'm going to grab drinks," Trick said after doing the same for Rylee. "Bellini?"

"White wine."

"No peaches for you, Peaches? What gives?"

The nickname prompted a raised eyebrow from Tripp. Dee gave him her order and the two men walked to the bar to collect the drinks.

"Sorry, I dove right in to asking Tripp about the cars before we sat down. I have no social graces when I'm off the clock."

"Are you ever off the clock?" Dee chuckled.

"Not really." Rylee shook her head abashedly. "I tend to quadruple check every item on my list. And then check once more."

"Hey, you're under a lot of pressure. This wedding is a big deal. Which begs the question, why don't you have, like five assistants?"

"I'm beginning to see the need for them," Rylee admitted. "In the past I've hired remote assistants to place orders and double-check stock and available dates, but with Ari and Ex being so famous, I didn't trust anyone to have their hands on this besides me, you and Tripp. And the other vendors, of course. They've been wonderful. Ex and Ari's wedding is by far the most extravagant wedding I've planned."

Which had had the added bonus of completely overwhelming Rylee. Maybe that was the real reason behind why she kissed Trick. She'd never behaved so out of character in her life—and while at work.

Dee must have noticed the worry tugging at the corner of Rylee's mouth. The other woman patted her hand. "Ari hired you because she knows your work ethic is unmatched. You have a gift for turning the ordinary into magical. And she trusts you because you have done everything in your power to make this event crease-free."

"I thought she hired me because I'm from Texas," Rylee sort of joked.

"Xavier loves that you're a Texan, but it's not mere geography that landed you this gig, sweetheart. Tripp and I see it too. You are a professional through and through. Everything is going to be perfect. You wouldn't allow it to be anything less."

"Thank you." Rylee meant it. A compliment from Dee went a long way.

"You're welcome." A smile tickled the corner of Dee's mouth as she checked the bar for the guys. "What's up with you making out with the enemy?"

Rylee turned her eyes to the ceiling before closing them and scrunching up her face. "I don't know how that happened. Trick is so different than I thought he was. He's kind, and thoughtful. He changed a tire today for a courier, and then filmed a video with her because she was a fan."

"That's sweet."

"Since he's agreed to film pre-wedding festivities, he's been around a lot. He continues to surprise me with brunch or snacks or offering to pick up a delivery. I didn't expect him to be this helpful. On his channel, he seemed, I don't know. *Different*."

"He's an entertainer. Not unlike Ari when she's in actress-mode. Or Xavier when he's touring for his latest book. Trust me, I understand what it's like to expect someone to be a certain way and having them surprise you."

Dee's smile warmed when she met eyes with Tripp across the room. "At first, I thought Tripp wasn't taking our assigned task as seriously as he should, but then I learned that he approaches problems from a different vantage point then me."

Rylee thought of Patrick mentioning his ADHD, and considered her own assumptions. He gleefully followed his impulses whereas she tended to plan everything out before attempting.

"Opposites attract," Dee said with a twinkle in her eye. "Don't underestimate how hot it can be between the sheets." Dee whispered that last part at the same time a glass of white wine was placed in front of Rylee.

Busted, she straightened her spine as Trick sat next to her with a beer. He started talking to Tripp about the ranch, and soon enough Dee was pulled into the conversation as well.

Rylee admired Patrick's ability to win over everyone he met. Even her, and she would have thought herself immune to a guy like him. In the end, it hadn't taken much for him to win her over to his side.

She thought about their explosive kiss and considered what Dee had said about how good their differences might play out in the bedroom. For the first time, Rylee considered taking a page from Trick's playbook and not planning ahead for a change. She sipped her wine and watched him through her lashes.

Tonight, she'd see where the evening took her. Or, more aptly, where it took *them*.

Eight

Rylee waved goodbye to Tripp and Dee as they made their way to the exit. She was feeling more relaxed than she had earlier, which was typically a warning sign. Staying vigilant was the only way to keep from overlooking pertinent details.

A quick glance at her watch showed that it was after six o'clock, well past quitting time for the average nine-to-five American, but for a wedding planner of a famous couple whose wedding was three days away…

"Whoa, whoa." Patrick gripped her shoulder. "You were loose and happy a second ago, but now you look as if a ghost walked over your grave."

"One very well might have. I never take this much time off so close to the wedding day." She looked around the bar, as nervous as if Ari and Ex were standing in the corner, ready to scold her. "It's criminal."

"Stealing light bulbs from the Cattleman's Club is criminal," Trick corrected. "Having a drink after a long day is merely human."

"You're in your own world. Has anyone ever told you that?"

"Almost everyone has told me that." His easy smile suggested he'd taken criticism lightly in the past. Not that she'd meant it that way. His lifestyle was enviable at times. "Lucky for you, you're in my world now."

"I thought you were in mine."

"Oh, I am. But afterhours? That's squarely in my realm." He lifted her wineglass by the stem. A scant amount of warm liquid sat in the bottom of the glass. "You've been nursing this for an hour. Let me freshen it up for you. One more?"

She opened her mouth to say she couldn't. That she had to go back to the TCC office and gather her laptop, and then go up to her room and work in bed until two in the morning. She wasn't sure what changed her mind, but thought it might have something to do with the eager anticipation in Trick's eyes. She wanted to tell him yes, as she'd told him yes several times before.

"I'm concerned by how easily you talk me into things," she said.

"Happens to the best of them, Rylee. No sense fighting enjoying yourself." His grabbed his empty mug as well. "Enjoyment is what life's about."

He was back from the bar in a blink with a fresh, chilled glass of chardonnay for her and another beer for him. She held the wine in her mouth for a second, savoring its oaky, buttery flavor.

"I do need to collect my things from the office tonight," she said, unable to let go of the idea completely.

"Why?" He appeared sincerely perplexed, which made her laugh out loud.

"Because the wedding—"

"Is Saturday. I know. For argument's sake, let's say none of those feathery pens work."

Her blood went as cold as her wine.

"Yep, you heard me. The guests show up, pluck the pens out and set them to the guest book to write their autographs." His eyes widened in faux horror. "And then *nothing* comes out. Not a single drop of ink. Now what?"

"I—I don't know." Worry rippled through her.

"I *do* know. You will break into the maintenance closet—definitely in your wheelhouse—and pilfer a box of Bic stick pens. Black, red, blue. Whatever you can find."

"*Red*?" Unacceptable. The panic must have shown on her face. He reached up and smoothed the wrinkle from her brow with his thumb.

"No one will care. Not Ari. Not Ex. Not the guests. Roll with what life throws you sometime, and watch what happens. You heading off every potential problem isn't what keeps the world spinning, Peaches. It does that on its own."

"I wish I could be spontaneous." She swallowed a gulp of her wine and tried to shake off the idea of red ink on the crisp white pages of the gold guest book. *Appalling.*

"Planner through and through, huh?"

"And back around and through again."

He laughed. She liked hearing him laugh. Liked the way it crinkled the corners of his eyes and loosened his posture. She noticed she was sitting ramrod straight and purposely tried to relax her own posture. It was easier to do while wearing the flat sandals she'd changed into after the high heel snapped off one of her pumps. She'd stashed the spare pair of shoes in her bag in case of emergency this morning. One point for her for planning ahead.

"How'd you start wedding planning, anyway? And don't give me a phone-it-in 'It's what I'm good at' answer. I want the real story."

"That's going to require a lot more wine."

"I can arrange for that." He moved to stand and she put her hand on his arm to stop him. Warmth from his skin transferred to her palm. He was so much more attractive than when she'd first spotted him in Royal. Maybe because she knew him better now.

He folded his arms on the table in front of his beer. "C'mon, Peaches. No one is here but us. It's completely off the record. Unless you still don't trust me."

"It's not that," she blurted out before she thought about it. Oddly enough, she *did* trust him. He'd been nothing but accommodating and agreeable. Plus, she liked finding out more about him. He operated so differently from her. He was sort of fascinating. "But if I tell you, you have to tell me something juicy about yourself."

"You mean like my wedding conquests past?"

"Ew."

"I'm joking." He gave her another of those broad, crinkly smiles that made her belly clench and her face heat. His sincere expression towed her in when he amended, "I'll tell you something I've never told anyone. How about that?"

As stoic as Rylee appeared on the outside, she *loved* secrets. Intrigued, she pursed her lips. Trick's gaze zoomed in on her mouth. She licked her bottom lip, watching as he shifted in his seat. A zing of awareness flitted through her veins.

While her past wasn't a topic she typically

discussed, she was aware that the situation with Trick was far from typical. Tucking a strand of hair behind her ear, she warned him with three words. "Are you ready?"

"Born that way." He grinned. "Hit me."

"Okay. Here goes."

Trick leaned in, expecting to hear a tale of a young, spunky, headstrong Rylee Meadows. Picturing her diving into the unknown excited him in a way that felt almost foreign. While he generally lived life flying by the seat of his pants, the women in his life rarely "excited" him in a way other than the physical. Rylee was a bold-faced exception to that rule. Not that he wasn't physically attracted to her—he could hardly keep his mind off kissing her again—but he was also insatiably curious about her.

"I grew up in a country club, don't-lift-a-finger household, I was taught that becoming a wife was the penultimate goal. I'd been dating a man two years older than my twenty-two, but Louis seemed older. He'd graduated with a degree in business, and had lined up a lucrative spot at my family's company. President was in his future."

"A professional." Trick wasn't surprised. Everything about Rylee screamed that she should be married to a doctor or a lawyer. Or the president of a company. "Does he still work for your family's company?"

She nodded. That must suck.

"Anyway, my future was laid out for me. It wasn't one I chose. My parents were thrilled that their daughter was engaged to a man who could provide, and had come from good stock."

"Sounds sexy," he said with a dab of jealousy. He couldn't imagine referring to a significant other as "stock" but then he wasn't from her world, was he? No one had expected too much from him after he'd been diagnosed with ADHD.

He'd been raised in an upper middle-class neighborhood in LA. His mom and dad worked hard every day. While his younger sister had been encouraged to pursue college, their parents hadn't pressed Patrick in the same way. Cassie had gone from a high school student to a college student in a blink.

Trick had attended film school, but had found a career adjacent to movies. He'd always done his own thing, made his own choices.

"I didn't feel butterflies or sparks for Louis," Rylee continued, "but I remember how well he was liked. I'd known him for years. He was a country-club kid, too. Nearly everyone in our families' circles gushed over how "perfect" we were together, and how "beautiful" our future babies would be."

Trick swallowed a mouth full of beer to keep from offering criticism. This Louis guy sounded bland. Tepid. Unforgivably boring. He didn't know Rylee, but what he knew of her suggested that a cardboard cutout of a husband was the last thing she needed in her life. She deserved someone who would take care of her, not someone who expected *her* to take care of *him*.

"I took a few college classes, but didn't fully commit to a full-time curriculum. Just generals while I decided what I wanted to be when I grew up. By the time Louis proposed that summer, his mind was made up. I wouldn't work. He was making great money.

I was going to be a wife, a mom and live out the rest of my days in wedded bliss.

"I threw myself into planning our wedding. I consulted with multiple florists and reception sites, dance instructors, caterers, bakers. You name it. I loved the organization of it, and the lists." Her smile revealed both dimples. "Ah, the lists."

"Some things didn't change, I see."

"The lists stayed." She took another drink from her glass before she continued. "About eight months into our engagement, I'd started talking about wanting to go into event planning as a career. I had recently offered my services for a friend's baby shower, and another friend's birthday party. I had been bitten by the entrepreneur bug. Louis saw my working as beneath us. He wanted to be seen as the husband who provided for his wife, and he found it embarrassing that I would stoop to, as he put it, 'serve others'. Shortly after, he called off the engagement.

"That's the stupidest thing I've ever heard," Trick grumbled, disliking this Louis guy more and more by the second.

"I was sheltered. Everyone else thought

Louis was right for me, so why shouldn't I? I didn't know any better than to blindly accept the life presented to me on a silver platter."

He reached for her hand and stroked her fingers with his. "Your ex sounds like a complete troglodyte."

She surprised him by laughing. "He was more taciturn than caveman. I'm not sure he'd ever been passionate about anything before he was passionate about me *not* going into business for myself."

"I'm sorry." Trick meant it. It was a shitty reason to end a relationship.

"I was sad that it ended, but mostly I was angry. Do you know how many non-refundable deposits I'd paid? Which, yes, was Louis's money, but it felt so wasteful. I'd carefully vetted everyone from the band members to the sommelier. And now, because I was damn good at what I did, I was supposed to let it go to waste?"

Damn, Trick liked hearing her talk like this. With enough passion to blaze a fiery trail through the center of town. When she described her abilities and talents, she came alive. She gestured with her hands, pulled her shoulders back and elevated her chin. Rylee was proud of what she'd accomplished—then and now. She should be. No way in hell would Trick attempt to plan anything as complex as a celebrity wedding—no matter how much help he had doing it.

"A friend of mine ended up pregnant, and was in a rush to be married before our entire community was *scandalized.* Can you believe that? In our modern society?" Rylee rolled her eyes.

He could believe it. Modern society could, at times, be downright ancient when it came to traditions.

"I asked her if it would be strange for her to take my entire wedding package, since the arrangements were already made. Free of charge, of course. I offered to help her with the details. The only thing she had to do was show up in a white dress."

"And she said yes," he concluded.

Rylee held up a finger. "Not at first. She'd voiced concerns that I was heartbroken and would regret handing over my wedding plans. I assured her that while I wasn't happy about being dumped, I had known deep down that

Louis wasn't right for me. Eventually she said yes. If she hadn't, she would have run out of time to conceal her baby bump.

"The wedding was incredible and, ironically, suited to my friend's tastes. I thought I had been making choices based on what *I* liked, but I realized I had been making them based on what others expected of me. Now I make decisions based on my own needs. No one else's."

He admired her moxie. She could have gone the other way and abandoned her dreams and goals in order to stay married to that toad. Or she could have allowed her doomed engagement to make her doubt herself. Instead, she'd grown a Jack's beanstalk of a business from one humble little bean.

"At the reception for my friend's wedding, I was approached by her cousin and a bridesmaid about their future weddings. They wanted to hire me to be their planner. I agreed on the spot, had some business cards printed and started my business. I moved from Texas to LA, and have been working nonstop ever since."

"God, Rylee." Awed, he shook his head.

"What?" Her smile was tremulous.

"You're incredible."

Her fair skin stained pink. She looked down at her wineglass. "I traded a fiancé for a career. I don't know if that makes me incredible, but it does make me scrappy."

Hell yes, it did. He had friends who would curl up and die if they'd had a fiancée dump them a few months before the wedding. And he had at least one other friend who would have trashed his future rather than embrace the newfound freedom and the opportunity to grow.

Rylee had gone from being a distractingly attractive rule-follower to a plucky, do-whatever-it-takes woman. She was take-charge and in-charge. She might have started out following her family's plan for her life, but she'd ended up chasing her own dreams. He was enamored. Enthralled.

Turned on.

"So, there it is. My tale of a passionless engagement and recycled wedding plans. And now you know I'm one of the snobby rich." She cupped her wineglass but didn't drink from it.

She was waiting for him to make a joke, perhaps at her expense. Instead he did what he'd wanted to do since they sat down at this table.

He leaned in and kissed her.

Nine

One minute Rylee was trotting out the scandalous and sordid tale of how she'd ended up planning the Noble-Ramos wedding, and the next she was being kissed thoroughly by the man who'd intended to crash it.

Trick's hands were cupping her face as his lips moved softly but firmly over hers. He didn't invade her mouth, but instead teased her lips with the very tip of his tongue. Abruptly, he backed away, ending the kiss too soon.

He didn't let go of her right away. He lingered, peering into her very soul as his mouth spread into a cunning smile. A smile that had her nipples pebbling inside of her bra, and warmth gathering between her legs.

"You're so fucking sexy I can't stand it," he murmured, his voice husky. "Sorry to attack you, I just…couldn't help myself." His throat bobbed with a laugh as a slightly chagrined look crossed his features. As if he'd been overcome by her and had taken himself by surprise.

Same.

She liked that he hadn't been fully in control of his faculties. Passion had been in short supply in her life. Partially because she was raised in a prim and proper environment. Rarely had she seen her father offer more than a demure peck to her mother's cheek. Affection had been tempered in her household.

She glanced around the restaurant, half expecting someone to be gaping at her very public display of affection, but no one was paying attention.

"I'll refrain from further lip-locks until you give me permission," he promised. "Your turn."

"My turn?"

"I promised to tell you something no one else knows. Or you can ask me anything."

She put her hand to her head. She'd forgotten they were in the middle of a conversation. "Right. I, uh, lost my place."

Grinning, he eased back into his chair. He wore smugness well.

"Did you go to college?"

"Ah, a softball."

"We can start slow." The comment held a charge. She could practically feel the hum in the air between them.

"Slow is good for me, Peaches." He cleared his throat. "College. Yes. Film school, actually. The idea of becoming a filmmaker was a straight shot from childhood to now." He arrowed his arm out in front of him. "I always knew I wanted to be an entertainer. I connected with the films I watched as a kid. I've wound up in front of the camera, but my original goal was to be behind it."

"You're good at what you do. Although, I'm not a fan of pranks you used to pull in your older videos."

"Most of those were Todd's ideas. Not to

lay blame, but he's not here to defend himself, so let's blame him."

"Was he a friend from film school?"

"Yeah. He's a good guy. I drew the line at humiliating people. No one likes to be made fun of."

"Tell me about it." While she'd had a fairly secure childhood, she recalled plenty of times she'd felt set apart from her friends. Her best friend Monica had been a wisp of air compared to Rylee's curvaceous build. "I never managed to slim down to the size of my closest friends. A few well-meaning but hurtful comments are still embedded in my memory."

Trick's mouth pulled into a frown.

"You know, because of…" She mimed the shape of an hourglass with her hands. "I should have asked, but I didn't hurt you when I fell on you, did I?"

"Are you fucking kidding me?" His tone was sharp, disapproving.

"N-no. I mean, I did fall from a considerable height."

He leaned in closer. So close she could make out the stubble pressed deliciously against his jawline. "I can handle every neckbreaking curve and hairpin turn on your body, Rylee." He made a low appreciative sound in the back of his throat before blatantly checking her out. "You're perfect. Insanely, distractingly perfect."

She hadn't been fishing for a compliment, and as a result had no idea what to do with one. Since those tender teenage years, she had accepted her body type and size. Rejoiced in it. She was active, healthy. She was also proud of the way she looked. But it'd been a long time since she'd taken her clothes off in an intimate act. The idea of being naked with Trick sent a barrage of tingles over her skin. She wasn't nervous, but *excited*. She'd always been self-conscious around Louis. He hadn't outright criticized her, but neither had he openly praised her.

"I'm so comfortable around you," she told Trick, awestruck by the realization. "More than I was with my fiancé. That's strange."

"Is it?"

"I guess not. Everyone else is at ease around you. Charm is one of your gifts. You don't have to try at it."

"Believe me, Peaches, with you I'm trying. I'm holding back so I don't scare you off."

"Scare me off? Do I seem easily frightened to you?"

"Fuck, no! You seem like the type of woman who is burned once and doesn't allow a second chance. I am well aware that I'm on borrowed time."

"Accurate." They stared at each other, soaking in the possibility of more. At least, she hoped he was contemplating more. She sure as hell was.

"I bet you've decided never to get married."

She inclined her head. "You are correct."

"Never getting married but planning weddings for others."

"It's an updated version of *always the bridesmaid but never a bride*." She sipped her wine and then asked, "What about you? Is there wedded bliss in your future?"

"Definitely. I always wanted to share my life with someone else. Being alone sucks."

She laughed, finding his easy admission startling. She would have put money on him being a total playboy. "That's a rare opinion for a guy. Of the weddings I've planned, 'cold feet' on the part of the groom was a real and diagnosable affliction."

"Yeah? How many of them bailed?"

"One," she answered. "But he came back."

"Let me guess, you hunted him down and talked some sense into him."

"His brother, the best man, did most of the talking. But I was there to facilitate."

"Of course you were. You couldn't let a groom with cold feet wreck your plans."

"True story." She took a breath. "Louis never viewed our relationship as a partnership. It was always him on top with me bringing up the rear."

She heard the double entendre too late. Trick raised both eyebrows as she covered her cheeks with her hands in an attempt to cool them down. "Oh, my god. I can't believe I just said that."

"You said it, not me."

They both laughed. He was so easy to hang out with.

"I did. I can't believe it, but I did. Ugh. Let's talk about something else. Will you have a huge wedding?"

"I guess it depends on my bride, doesn't

it?" he asked, thoughtful. "But if I have a say, I've always pictured a wedding on a cliffside with, like, four people in attendance."

"My parents would die of culture shock if I dared to have a small wedding. Seeing and being seen is practically etched into our family crest."

"They wouldn't *die*. They recovered after you built a career rather than marry Mr. Personality, didn't they?"

"They are alive and well." Her smile was unstoppable. Her wine was also gone. For the first time in a long, long time, she wanted to order another glass and blow off her responsibilities. So, so tempting. Impossible, but tempting.

"You sound like you have good parents. They didn't give you too hard of a time about the wedding falling apart, did they?"

"No, actually. They were supportive. I wonder if they had second thoughts about Louis and his intentions. Though my mother would love to be bouncing a grandbaby on her hip right about now."

"Plenty of time for that."

"What are your parents like?"

"My dad is a mason and a complete jokester." He pointed to himself to show that he'd inherited that particular skill set. "My mom tried acting, but ended up a costume designer instead. She used to take me to the set with her. I fell in love with everything around me. It was a cool way to grow up."

"Sounds amazing." His upbringing was wild and unexpected whereas hers had been mapped-out and boxed-in. Had she grown into the woman her parents had cultivated, or had she chosen her own path? Spontaneity was a rare trait in the Meadows family. The idea that she'd been popped out of a mold of their making bothered her. Sure, she'd had a mostly good childhood, but no one wanted to believe they'd been crafted in a laboratory like Edward Scissorhands.

Trick polished off his beer and set the empty glass on the table. Their night was coming to a fast close.

"It's late." He checked his phone. Then he opened the app where literally millions of strangers followed him. What was it like to be admired by that many people?

"Did we go viral yet?" She didn't know

how she felt about being on his social media channel. Excited? Weird? Both?

"Not yet, but there are no shortage of comments." He lifted an eyebrow. "Most of them encouraging me to kiss you."

"They saw that coming."

"Guess so." He continued scrolling. "And—"

"Don't tell me any bad ones."

"There aren't any. But I have good moderators who delete them for me." He winked. "I was going to say that someone has offered to replace your shoes."

"Seriously?"

"Yup, and… I don't know if you want to know this."

"What? What is it?"

"There are a lot of peach emojis. A *lot*."

"Oh, god." She shielded her eyes. "In reference to my ass, I'm guessing."

"Well, I did refer to you as Peaches. But in their defense, you do have a fantastic ass, so probably." He chuckled, wily and wicked. Both of those attributes were doing it for her tonight. That was a first. "I assume you have to go back to your room soon."

As much as she hated to admit he was right,

she had a million things to do. Reluctantly, she pushed out of her seat and collected her purse. “It’s probably the best idea to call it a night.”

“Far from the best idea,” he argued as he stood with her. “I’ll walk you to your room.”

Ten

"Floor?" Trick asked as they entered the elevator.

"Six."

He pressed the button.

"Are you on six, too?"

"Four." He cleared his throat, uncharacteristically nervous. Rylee, unlike most people he encountered in his day to day, intimated the hell out of him. It wasn't her wealthy upbringing, either. Trick had been in the company of famous people on-and-off in his life. Hell, he'd crashed more than a few events where celebrities had been in attendance.

No, the intimidation factor with Rylee was

that he didn't want to blow his shot with her. He couldn't tell where her head was, and found himself guessing instead of knowing what she wanted. Confidence was his baseline, but she'd knocked him off balance. He'd been on the balls of his feet since she'd walked into his tailoring appointment.

They arrived on her floor. He stepped out of the elevator and walked with her in silence down a corridor. She turned right. He followed. Her room—a suite—was set apart from the other rooms for privacy. A note hung on the handle and she lifted it to read the message.

"My package arrived from Ariana. She sent me a gift. So thoughtful." Rylee slapped the notecard against her palm, a nervous gestured while lingering at the door. "Do you—"

"Yes." They'd had a phenomenal day, and evening, and he wasn't ready for it to be over.

"You don't know what I was going to ask," she said around bubbly laughter.

"Do I…want to see the gift? Do I want to have a nightcap? Do I want a kiss before I travel two lonely floors to my own room?" He shrugged. "All yeses."

"You'll get a kiss, at least, Trick." She let that tantalizing comment dangle like bait on a hook as she let them into her room. Correction, her *suite*. It was easily three times bigger than his own room in the Bellamy, with an office area, a living room, and of course, the bedroom. He followed her to the desk, glancing over at the crisp white comforter covering the bed mere feet away.

She opened the shiny black box wrapped in white ribbon to reveal a selection of products Ariana had chosen for her. "Wow, what an amazing selection. She picks the best stuff."

"Most lifestyle brands do." He grabbed a bottle of massage oil from the box. "Are you a fan of guava?" He showed her the label. "It's edible."

"Stop! Are you kidding?" She took the bottle and read the label for herself. Then she dug through the crinkle paper tucked around the products and held them up one by one. "A sleep mask, tea, a pocket massager. Exfoliating facial masks… What on earth did she expect me to do with these?"

"I instantly have a hundred and one ideas."

Every last one of them involved Rylee out of that dress and in his arms.

She fiddled with the elastic band on the black silk sleep mask. He half expected her to fling it at him, or playfully punch his arm. Instead, she stepped closer to him, invading his space with her soft floral sent and the bluest eyes he'd ever seen.

"Well?" She hoisted an eyebrow. A dare. He recognized this version of Rylee from their first kiss. And so, he threw her words back at her.

"What am I waiting for?"

"Exactly," she whispered.

Hand on the back of her neck, he towed her in. Unlike the kiss at the tapas bar, he didn't have to be polite. Without an audience, there was no need to cut the kiss short. He took his time, molding his lips to the shape of hers, drinking her in—an attempt to slake his thirst for her.

Not possible. But he was going to try.

She kissed him back, pressing her body to his, her breasts bumping his chest. He cupped her butt with one hand and gave the cheek a squeeze and she instinctively tipped her hips forward. She couldn't think of anything except how she wanted every part of him touching every part of her.

He smiled down at her. "Peaches."

"Don't make fun of me."

"I'd never." He dove back in and lit her on fire. His warm wet tongue stroked hers and she clinched her thighs. Partially to assuage the throbbing there. She had yet to stop imagining his mouth on her body. On *every part* of her body.

She wasn't typically plagued with sexual or even romantic fantasies. While she'd had a coffee date here or there, none of those dates had prompted the idea of a second. And the kisses, with Louis and since, had been forgettable. A blur of gray.

There was nothing "gray" about Trick. He was fiery red and burnished orange, sunny yellow… She was awash in summery tones as heat saturated her bloodstream. His tongue stroked hers, and she emitted a helpless whimper.

He tightened his hold on her ass and pressed her hips to his. They lined up too well. His hardness, her softness. The levity dancing in his dark eyes had shifted to molten desire. He watched her from beneath drowsy lids as he said, “Give me the mask.”

She’d forgotten she was holding the sleep mask. Black silk with a tiny diamond star in one corner. He took it from her and then reached for her hair clip, letting her fair hair fall into loose waves. Then he covered her eyes with the mask.

She felt his breath against her lips when he invited, “Ready to have some fun?”

“Overdue,” she breathed, only half joking but pleased when she heard his raspy laugh.

“God, I hear you.”

She assumed his dry spell wasn’t as kindling-like as her own. Ever since she’d dared him to kiss her today, she’d been justifying to herself that it was okay to like him. More out of habit than anything else. No one had demanded she explain herself. Hell, Dee had practically told her to go for it after her own opposites-attract love story had turned out so well.

Which was *not* what this was about with Patrick, Rylee reminded herself. He was from an entirely different world than she was. She was in no danger of falling in love with him. Trick was a good-time guy, and he was willing to have a good time with her. For once she didn't want to plan and overthink.

He grasped her hand and lead her in the direction of the bedroom before backtracking to rifle through the box she'd opened.

"We're going to need some of this stuff," he said. "Hell, maybe all of it."

Her heart thrashed excitedly as he walked her from the suite to the bedroom. She felt heat emanating from his body when came around to stand before her. She heard him toss the box aside.

"Changed my mind." He removed her mask. She blinked, her eyes adjusting to the dim light of the room. "I want to see those blues."

He kissed her again, but his hands didn't stay in one place. They roamed, down her ribs and up again, where they cupped her breasts as his thumbs played over her nipples. They were peaked to the point of pain, begging to be free from the bra she'd worn for way too long today. As if in answer to her silent request, he drew down the zipper of her dress. Inch by agonizing inch, he opened the back of the garment and then smoothed the sleeves off her shoulders. His lips left hers to place a soft kiss on the top of one shoulder, and then he flicked open the front clasp of her bra.

"Tell me your nipples are peach-colored too and I'll die a happy man." He parted the material of her bra and cupped her generous D-cups with his palms. "Goddamn, Rylee. You are so fucking beautiful."

He suckled one nipple into his mouth, swirling it with his tongue as his fingers plucked the other. She gripped a handful of his thick hair, arching her back in response to the sharp pleasure spiking between her legs.

He raised his head, barely giving her a chance to take a breath before he lowered his mouth to the other nipple and sent her on a repeat journey.

"I knew you'd taste good everywhere." He freed her from the bra straps and then dropped her dress to the floor. On his knees in front of her, he took her shoes off one by one. "To be sure, though, I have more exploring to do."

He peered up at her, on his knees, his eyes hooded, his smile lazy but confident. He was still completely dressed, which seemed unfair since she was only wearing her underwear. He tucked his fingers into the waistband of those next, complimenting her on the pale pink color that matched her discarded bra. He rolled them down, past her thighs. She shifted her hips, excited and nervous in equal amounts. Once she'd stepped out of her panties, he held one foot in the air and gently draped her leg over his shoulder. Now she was open to him, the crook of her knee hooked on his shoulder, her center open to his perusal.

He took a long look as her heart hammered and her fingernails dug into his shoulder. Then, his hazel eyes on hers, he leaned forward and dragged his tongue along her folds.

"Oh, god." She hadn't meant to speak. The slick, wet feel of his tongue on her most sensitive part had drawn the words from her without her permission. She continued moaning as she rode his mouth—that talented mouth—

musing that he was every bit as good at this as she'd assumed he would be when he'd kissed her.

His hands roamed, one cupping her ass, the other reaching up to play with her nipple, hardening in the air-conditioned room. He plucked and laved in tandem while she moaned her approval. She said his name a few times, and "oh, god" a few more times. The rest of what she uttered was nonsensical gibberish. She was beyond caring. Nothing had felt this good. *Ever.*

Her orgasm shimmered on the horizon, growing closer like a speeding train on the tracks. It came into view, glimmering in the moonlight, and she voiced it with a long, appreciative moan. With her hands in his hair, she rode out her release, weakened by the sheer strength of it.

Trick held tightly to her thighs as he savored every moment of her release. He finally relented when she weakly begged for him to stop. She was swept up into his arms and then being lowered onto the bed. Her body sank into the pillowy white comforter while her mind floated miles above it. Part of her was lost in the afterglow. It pulsed through her, keeping time with her heavy heartbeats.

She flopped an arm over her closed eyes, mumbled something about how gifted he was, and then his mouth was on hers. When he moved her arm aside, he was the very picture of a smug male who had done exactly what he'd set out to do.

"Let's hear it," he said. "Scale of one to ten."

"A million?"

His sexy grin broadened. It was high time he removed the clothing he was still wearing. Weakly, she plucked at his shirt. "Take that off. I'm too tired."

"Yes, ma'am." He stood and pulled the shirt over his head, revealing a sculpted chest with a tasteful smattering of hair in all the right places. His pecs were round and thick, his biceps impressive, but then she'd been ogling those earlier, hadn't she? She refocused on his abs, the smooth bumps that led to a belly button and a trail of wiry hair that disappeared past his belt.

"Those, too." She snapped her fingers for effect. He gave her a stern look, which still managed to look playful on him, and then undid the belt and lost the pants. She didn't have to lecture him about taking off the boxer briefs. He slipped out of those too, freezing the next command on her tongue in its tracks.

His cock was tall and proud, grazing the top of his belly. He reached for it, gave it one stroke, then two, and her mouth literally watered. She couldn't look away. It was like seeing a sunset for the first time. Or a unicorn. My god, it was beautiful. Thick, too, which made her thighs squeeze together in delicious anticipation.

"We have more to do before the finale, Peaches." He crawled onto the bed and laid next to her. She rolled over to argue, reaching for the appendage she wanted inside of her as of two minutes ago.

He snatched her hand away and pinned it to the pillow over her head. He repeated that move with her other hand. Once he was over top of her, told her the score. "First the mask. And then the massage oil. Maybe that vibrating thing."

She bit her lip with her top teeth.

"No one wears a *yes* the way you do, Rylee." He kissed her on the lips, instructed her not to move, and then he grabbed the oil.

Eleven

Trick had focused his massaging techniques on her nipples since the oil was edible. It didn't taste half bad. Although he supposed when slicked over those peach, pert points, any flavor would have sufficed.

The mask covered her eyes, and her hands rested over head as he'd instructed. Each time he backed away to look at her body spread out before him like a goddamn dessert, her breathing would increase ever so slightly.

Rylee Meadows was *not* used to being out of control.

He'd enjoyed how she'd let go with him. How she'd said yes to him when her first instinct had been to turn him down. How she'd relinquished control tonight. Done with the oil, he tracked his fingers over her body, starting with her arms and then to the breasts he wanted to build an altar to worship.

"You have the most gorgeous breasts." He touched each of her nipples and watched as they tightened. Her body responded to him instantly, which was the most amazing thing. "And thighs."

He gripped each thigh with his hands and then spread her legs open. Forget the massager. He wanted to touch her here.

"Can I see you now?" Her hands were free, but she didn't remove the mask. Seemed as if the woman who was in charge of everything was reveling in the opportunity to be told what to do. He could understand that. He'd watched her, even from afar, as she'd planned and scheduled, delegated and answered. If he had her career, he'd need a vacation every other *week*. The worst part was, she hadn't enjoyed the parties she'd planned, but stayed at the ready in case something went wrong.

No fun.

He took the mask off. Her gaze went straight

to his dick, the hunger in her eyes unmistakable. She pushed herself up, her smile wonky and relaxed, her cheeks rosy. Then she sat up and pushed him onto his back. He let her, easing onto the bed and propping one arm behind his head.

"I'm not the only buffet in town, buddy." God, she was cute on her knees in front of him. Especially while lowering her mouth to his favorite part of his body. She lifted his erection, painfully hard at this point, and circled the head with her tongue. Then she took him into her mouth and he said a quick thank-you that she hadn't tried to make him wear the mask. Missing out on watching her plush pink lips take him in and slide away would have been a crime.

He swore as he palmed her flaxen head. His fingers stroked and then clutched when she swallowed him down again, leaving nowhere for him to go—not that he wanted to be anywhere else. She let him loose with a *pop*, then sat back on her knees, resting her palms on her thighs. Her large perky breasts beckoned, so he pushed himself up to meet her.

"I wasn't done yet."

"Oh, you're done." He reversed their positions, her beneath him, those dimples punctuating her cheeks as a throaty laugh exited her lush mouth. He kissed her and then left in search of his pants, where he hoped to god there was a condom. He opened his wallet, said a prayer and—*yes*! Actually, he said it out loud.

"I hadn't thought that far ahead and you have one in your wallet?"

He checked the expiration date. "Yeah. Still good, too."

"Well that's a relief. I was about to call the front desk."

"No need." He tore open the condom, amused to notice that his hands were shaking as he eased it over his aching girth. Steadying his breathing, he positioned himself over top of her. "I'm going to try my best to last as long as you—*Fuck*."

She didn't let him finish his promise before she guided his cock deep inside her channel. Surrounded by tight warmth, he again vowed to last as long as she needed him to.

"I don't care about long. I care about *hard*. Can you deliver?"

"Yeah. I can deliver on hard." Sweat broke out on his forehead as he lifted her right leg and rested her knee in the crook of his elbow. Angling her so that he was seated deeper, he thrust forward. "Can you handle me?"

Lust had widened her dark pupils, black eating up the surrounding blue. Her mouth had dropped open, her "yes" a barely audible breath.

"I thought you could." He was beginning to think she could handle absolutely anything. He hated the idea of her trussed up for some stiff who had only wanted a trophy wife. That wasn't her. Rylee was spirited, sexy, wild.

She was *his*.

The thought came, but he didn't push it away. He didn't question it, didn't evaluate it. He'd learned a long time ago that his instincts were a lot smarter than he was.

He started with slow, easy thrusts before graduating to harder, faster. Soon he was slamming into her, the rhythm hectic, desperate. Winded, he released her leg and dropped his hands to the mattress. She wrapped her legs around his waist and her arms around his neck, trapping him there.

"There, there. You feel *so* good," she praised. He worked her into a moaning, squirming lather, each of her compliments going straight to his dick.

"Come, Rylee," he demanded. "Right now."

"Again?"

"Yeah, honey. Again." He reached between their bodies and set his thumb to her clit, adding pressure as he stroked into her, filling her, working her exactly the way she needed to be worked.

Her forehead creased in pleasure-meets-pain pleats. A second later, she scratched her nails across his shoulders and cried out. Embedded deep within her, he felt her inner muscles spasm around him, pulling his own orgasm from him in one long, mind-altering release.

Eyes squeezed shut, he nearly blacked out from pleasure. He rode out the final waves of his release, lost in a sea of sensations. His mind was empty. His arms were full of Rylee. He sucked in a labored breath and some of her hair with it, pulling it off his tongue and kissing her neck instead.

Her arms closed around him while and he

laid, silent and still, willing himself, despite feeling as if he was in an entire field full of poppies, *not* to fall asleep.

"Slap me."

Since Trick had murmured that into her neck, Rylee wasn't sure she'd heard him correctly. "What did you just say?"

Eyes closed, he lifted his head and said, "Slap me so I don't fall asleep. I'll never forgive myself if I do." Then those eyes opened and he kissed her firmly on the mouth. "Kidding. But seriously if I start looking sleepy, do it."

Her laughter had never been so carefree.

"Let me take care of this." He kissed her and climbed from the bed. She hugged her pillow and watched his backside flex in the lamplight. Then she sighed to herself, content.

When was the last time she'd felt this comfortable after a physical romp? The answer was swift: *never.* She'd never felt this way with Louis. He'd been the only sexual encounter she'd had, save for a few second-base experiences.

Since Louis was her first =, she'd had no one to compare him to. Now that she'd had a ten-on-the-Richter-scale orgasm, her ex was faring far worse than she'd known. Trick was attentive and, more importantly, *fun*.

Planning weddings might look fun on the outside, but that wasn't the word she'd use to describe her career. Rewarding, yes. Profitable, absolutely. Nothing was as satisfying as helping someone else's dreams come true. But, her vocation had come with a price. Sleepless nights and working every weekend, which made getting together with friends challenging.

When Trick had arrived in Royal, she'd been convinced he was going to ruin Ari and Ex's wedding, and Rylee's reputation by proxy. Instead, he'd been agreeable and helpful. And had taken her from a woman on a mission to a woman in the missionary position.

She chuckled at her own joke as he returned from the bathroom. Gloriously naked and completely confident, he strutted toward her.

"I love that smile." The box Ari had sent was on the dresser. He rummaged through it.

"There's more in here we can take advantage of tonight." He unearthed a flat gold box she must have overlooked. "Chocolate?"

He plopped onto his side on the bed, the open box of chocolates between them. He lifted a piece of dark chocolate from its brown crinkly wrapper. "Chocolate roulette. Sure I know it's dark, but anything could be inside. Cream. Coconut." He made a face. "Baked beans."

"Let's hope not," she said through a laugh. Tugging the sheet so that it covered her breasts, she rolled to her side to face him. She closed her eyes and picked a chocolate. They said "cheers" and tapped the candies together before each taking a bite.

"Chocolate cream." She hummed her approval as she chewed.

"Mine's filled with toothpaste. How disappointing."

She almost choked on another laugh , but managed to pull herself together. They polished off one more chocolate apiece, coconut for her and vanilla crème for him.

"Will you change your mind about crashing weddings after this weekend? Or did I ruin your streak since you are technically invited to this one?"

"That award goes to Esther Edmonton." He picked through the chocolates and came out with a small square-shaped piece.

"Who is Esther Edmonton?"

"She's a saucy grandmother I met last year at a wedding I crashed. She asked me to dance with her, assuming I was one of the groom's friends. What could I do?"

"Nothing. Clearly. You were trapped."

"She knew it, too." He ate the candy and sucked a bit of melted chocolate off his thumb. She stared for a prolonged beat, parts of her growing warm at the idea of where his mouth had been tonight. "She used to be a nurse. She told me she was married fifty-two years to a 'wonderful man' who she couldn't wait to see again in heaven."

Rylee put a hand over her heart. "Aww."

"It gets better. Esther regretted never having her own children, so she said she hoped her grandniece—the bride—chose to 'make babies' with her husband. Then she asked me if I'd like to 'make babies' and I told her I was flattered, but I was much too young to consider a family with a woman so out of my league." Rylee giggled on cue. "And then I gave her the real answer. I told her I'd love to have kids, but I'm in no rush."

Rapt, she leaned in.

"Then I asked Esther if I could interview her on camera and we sat and talked for another forty minutes in a quiet corner of the reception hall. I never put the footage up. It felt private, you know?"

He picked another chocolate out of the box and offered it to her. She took it, but didn't eat it right away. "I'm afraid you're about to tell me something sad."

"I am." He offered a tight smile. "The bride—Brittany— contacted me after she found footage of me at her wedding. In the email, she said her great-aunt Esther had passed away. Apparently, Esther had mentioned me multiple times since the wedding, and the fact that she'd been interviewed. Brittany sought out my channel hoping that I'd posted the interview. I explained that I'd kept it private, but I was happy to send it to her." He took a breath before continuing, obviously saddened about Esther's passing. Rylee could understand why. She felt sad too and had never met the woman. "Anyway. I edited a video together and sent it to Brittany. There were so many great moments, little moments that are normally edited out. Those are the best parts. Esther looking off to the side. Losing her train of thought and laughing. Telling me a dirty joke."

Tears in her eyes, Rylee smiled.

"I knew the moment I finished that edit and emailed it off that I was in the wrong business. I had taken a left when I should have hung a right. I started out in film school for a reason, and it had nothing to do with followers, sponsorships or blocking comments from trolls. Ironically, had I not crashed that wedding, I never would have met Esther and found my way, you know?"

"So, what now?" The story couldn't end there.

"I'm in deep, Peaches. Like when someone is in the mob. I have sponsorships I've agreed to that I either need to honor or cancel. I have a video schedule to adhere to, although I'm looking into crashing celebrity charity events to spotlight the charity rather than myself. It's a pivot, for sure. Slower than I'd like, but I've never been patient."

"So, you're going to be a filmmaker after all? Documenting the small moments in life."

"The best moments are the moments that are usually edited out of the final." He picked another chocolate out of the box and tossed it into his mouth. "Like the one we're having now."

Twelve

When her alarm jangled from her phone on the nightstand, Rylee launched out an arm to tap the Stop button like she did nearly every morning at 6 a.m. Instead of her phone, she encountered a muscular male arm. A rogue dart of panic stabbed her chest for a fraction of a second before she recalled the night before.

Trick following her to her room. The basket of self-care goodies from Ari reimagined as props for foreplay. The incredible sex. Eating chocolate in bed. Him mentioning how life was made up of little moments that were often edited out to allow the bigger moments to shine.

"Sorry," she whispered, reaching past him for her phone.

He muttered under his breath. Then his arm lashed around her back and he tugged her roughly against his naked body. His mouth hit her neck and she felt his lips tickle her skin when he rumbled, "Morning."

But that wasn't all she felt. Several inches of morning wood pressed against her when he shifted his hips. This was definitely an improvement from how she normally awoke each morning. She dropped her phone back onto the nightstand and reached beneath the blankets. She gripped his erection, massaging it once, twice.

He responded by thrusting into her hand as he yanked the covers off both of them. Then he removed her hand and kissed her palm before kissing his way down her body. He paused to flick his tongue over each nipple and her belly button before settling between her legs.

"Trick." Whatever excuse she was about to make about being late was lost on a sigh. She rested her hands on his head, tangling her fingers in his messy hair. The room was dark thanks to the heavy curtains being pulled. Her alarm was off. It was too early for anyone to call with an emergency. She further reasoned that she made her own schedule, and she could do whatever she damn well pleased. Her brain tried to insert a to-do list into the mix, but the man between her thighs must have sensed he was about to lose her. He doubled his efforts, effectively erasing any coherent thought from her head.

Mere minutes later, an orgasm slammed into her without warning, wringing a cry from her lips.

"You're so fucking hot." He bit the inside of her thigh and soothed it with a kiss.

She ruffled his hair, thinking to herself that it was Trick, not her, who was hot. With his dark hair a mess, his five o'clock shadow scraping her sensitive skin, and those hooded eyes that tempted her to laze around all day with him, he was sexy as hell. Add that up with last night and what he'd just done to her? Forget it. He was her ultimate fantasy man.

"How many more do you want?" Her fantasy man's gaze was on her face when he slid his tongue over her clit.

"Do you charge by the hour?"

"By the orgasm, in your case. It doesn't take an hour to start you up, Peaches."

"Ugh." She covered her face in her hands. "More proof I don't know what I'm doing when it comes to one-night stands."

He shifted positions so quickly, she was face-to-face with him in a blink. "What are you talking about?"

"You're my first."

"Your first." An alarmed expression crossed his handsome features.

"Not my first *time*. My first one-night stand."

"Oh." Relief, and then he shook his head. "That's not what this is, Rylee."

"Of course it is. I mean, I know it's morning instead of night, but we're within a twenty-four-hour window."

"I'm in town for a few more days." His eyebrows drew together over his nose. "You're not escaping me that easily. I'm your partner, remember?"

"That was your term, I believe." She kept

her tone light, but she was surprised to hear he wanted more than one night. "I'm going to be busy with the final preparations, you know."

"You're also going to be getting busy *with me*." She liked the hint of possessiveness in his voice way too much. "How else can you expect to work off the stress that builds on any given day. He gripped her thigh and massaged it gently. Don't you want to keep your heart healthy? I can help with that." He pressed a kiss between her breasts, right over her fluttering heart. "Last night, tonight, tomorrow, and the wedding night makes this a *four*-night stand."

"I'm not sure we can include the wedding night. I'm usually ready to collapse by then. Don't expect any acrobatics."

He kissed her nipple succinctly and then looped her leg around his hip. "You like to point out your limitations. When are you going to realize I'm far more capable, patient and talented than your country-club boyfriend?"

Oh, she'd already realized that. She played with Trick's unkempt hair, loving the way it stubbornly flopped to one side, refusing to be tamed. A good metaphor for him. Where her ex-boyfriend had been as tame as a pony at a children's birthday party, Trick struck her as a man who couldn't be corralled. Plus, what was the harm in a four-night stand? They were already in Royal together—in the same hotel, no less. It would be silly to stop sleeping together, especially since he didn't want to stop. Frankly, neither did she.

"So, you're not done? With me," she couldn't help pointing out, a hint of disbelief in her tone.

"Peaches." His grin was feral, infectious. "I'm just getting started."

Trick was a lighthearted guy, but it still surprised him when he began whistling his way through the lobby of the Bellamy. That was new.

He passed the tapas bar, smiling as he recalled last night. He had hoped the evening would end with Rylee in his bed—or his in hers, he hadn't been picky—but the resulting night he'd spent having sex with her, laughing with her, and confessing his secret motivation for changing careers had been unexpected.

And not in a bad way.

After they'd sorted out that one-night stand dilemma, he'd made love to her again, effectively silencing any argument she might have made that she would be late for work. She worked too much. Her focus was always on others and not on herself. She deserved a break. He'd talked her into giving him an hour. Incredible sex plus a long hot shower had eaten up that hour up and then some. She'd admonished him, but the smile on her face had never gone away.

He'd promised to make up for lost minutes by picking up coffee, and then he'd dashed down to his room to get dressed. She'd assured him she could be ready in fifteen minutes and would meet him in the lobby. He knew she was organized and punctual, but fifteen minutes was a feat that remained to be seen.

There was a fancy coffee kiosk adjacent to the lobby where an eager barista awaited his approach. He'd expected more people to be in line, but perhaps the Bellamy's residents had taken advantage of the in-room coffee makers instead.

Their coffees in to-go cups, one in each hand, he was angling for a sofa when the elevator doors pinged and opened. Out stepped the woman he hadn't known he'd been dreaming of until he'd set foot in the great state of Texas.

Her super short black dress gave him a stellar view of the legs he'd enjoyed having wrapped around his neck this morning. Her shoes were tall with a lot of straps. Even as he thought she must be swearing with every step she took, he appreciated how damn sexy they were. How damn sexy she looked wearing them. Her confidence accompanied every sharp heel tap, the short ruffly sleeves of the dress lifting in the breeze she made on her way to him.

"I didn't think you could pull off fifteen minutes."

"I have my routine down." She adjusted her purse on her shoulder and smiled, gifting him with those cute dimples. "Plus, I left everything in the office at the TCC yesterday, so I didn't have anything to pack up".

She pushed her bangs off her forehead. Her mid-length, pale blond hair was down in loose waves. Had she run out of time to pin it back? Or had he put her into a loose, relaxed mood that her hairstyle was reflecting? He liked the idea that he could be partly responsible for her literally letting her hair down. He also hoped he'd had something to do with the spring in her step and the bright smile on her beautiful face.

"I didn't think you could look any better than you did naked next to me in bed." He handed over her coffee as she jerked her eyes around the practically empty lobby. "I was right. You look better naked. But you still look amazing."

"Just when I think you're going to be serious." She shook her head, but she didn't appear the least bit upset that he'd teased her.

"I'm completely serious. Do you need me to go over which body parts are my favorite? Which sounds you make that I like best? What about—" She pressed her fingers to his lips, something she'd done before. He smiled against her fingertips, kissing them lightly before she pulled them away. "What's on our agenda today?"

"The usual. Planning a wedding."

They walked into the parking lot to her mother's car that she'd borrowed for the week. On the short drive to the TCC, Rylee detailed the "ten million things" she had to do before the wedding on Saturday.

The list made him instantly fatigued. He took a deep drink of his coffee, glad he'd gone for an extra shot of espresso. His agenda wasn't so much an agenda with a timeline and bullet-pointed tasks—he shuddered—than him waiting for the right moment to turn on the camera. After filming for years, he had a sixth sense about what to shoot and what angles were best. He operated on instinct, not pragmatism. Too much planning gave him hives.

"And then the rehearsal dinner tonight, of course."

Shit! He'd forgotten about that. She caught his alarmed expression as she parked near the side entrance.

"You forgot."

"I didn't. Okay, I did, but I would have remembered way before that."

"Don't worry. You will have a break late afternoon to go back to your room and freshen up if you need to." She patted his cheek. He caught her hand. They sat in her car, keys off, the interior heating in the Texas sun, staring into each other's eyes. Her blues exactly matched the clear sky. Unbidden, the moment took on a different vibe. Serious. *Meaningful.* One of those moments in life that is not to be missed for other seemingly more important ones. To keep from wading into the deep end far too soon, he rerouted the conversation to sex.

"Not unless you come to my room with me. We didn't use every item in that gift box, you know."

"You're not going to waste a single second while you're here, are you?" The question was rhetorical, he assumed, since she left him in the car rather than wait for him to answer.

He shut his car door and followed her to the building, the strangest sensation spreading over his chest. What had started out as mind-blowing sex with the wedding planner who'd been his nemesis for the last few months had changed into something more.

And without his permission.

Did they…have a future? A terrifying prospect for a guy who rarely planned ahead. The premonition didn't fade for a good hour or two. He tried not to obsess over what that might mean.

Thirteen

Her morning had started with a bang. Not only was she on the phone answering questions from the caterers about table settings, but while she was on the phone, Ariana had sent texts.

Multiple texts.

For good reason, Rylee calmly reminded herself as she took a deep breath. She'd asked Ari to let her know of any last-minute seating changes so that Rylee could let the caterer know. A cancellation or an additional plus-one was to be expected. What Rylee hadn't expected was *seven* additional guests and a request from a couple in the middle of a divorce to sit at different tables. Now the entire seating plan was thrown off.

"Here we have our cool under pressure wedding planner," Trick narrated. He'd warned her he'd be filming this morning. She forced an amiable smile for the camera, but on the inside she was Edvard Munch's *The Scream*.

Rylee had already phoned the calligrapher, who'd thankfully answered. The bad news was, she was out of town. As in *Germany*. Rylee couldn't very well demand that the woman stay in the States until after the wedding, but she wondered if she should make that request in the future.

She had explained the seating kerfuffle, asking the calligrapher to pen, scan and email the files. Rylee would figure out a way to print them onto Ari's and Ex's specialty card stock so that they matched the others. Unfortunately, the calligrapher had just boarded her flight and would be staying in a small town without Wi-Fi as part of a "digital cleanse." Rylee had been tempted to swear or beg or cry—or a combination of the three—but in the end had wished the other woman a happy vacation.

Trick swept the camera over the reception area, pointing out the large chandeliers and the dance floor. He mentioned that Colin Reynolds, Irish-born head chef for the local restaurant, Sheen, would be catering.

Rylee shook her head in bemusement as she thought back to her mini meltdown a few months ago. When she'd been wishing Trick would have chosen any event other than hers. Now, she didn't wish that. She found his presence, including his attention to the details she'd so carefully orchestrated with the vendors, soothing.

It was funny how drastically her feelings had changed.

He signed off and tucked the phone into the pocket of his pants. He wore pale-colored trousers today with a deep green T-shirt that complemented his black hair and olive complexion. She no longer saw the wedding crasher hell-bent on destroying her world, she saw the man with his head on her hotel pillow grinning back at her.

It blew her mind that she'd become comfortable being naked with him in such a short period of time, but maybe it shouldn't. Trick wooed everyone within shouting distance, and since he was online daily, that was a lot of people.

A lot of *women*.

Frowning at the rogue streak of jealousy, she quickly slapped on the smile she'd worn for the camera a moment ago.

"What's up?" He narrowed his eyes in suspicion. "I can tell you're faking being happy. You're practically wearing your shoulders as earrings." He placed his palms on her shoulders and gently pushed them down. His touch, his unerring eye contact, and that sideways smirk hinting that everything would be okay calmed her some. "Talk to me, Peaches. Who ruined your day already?"

"The calligrapher," she answered, relieved to have someone to talk to about it. She recapped the seating-chart tragedy and waited for his face to reflect her defeat. That didn't happen, of course. He was Patrick MacArthur, man capable of only good moods.

"Who else can write names on parchment that you know?"

"It's not that simple. They must match *exactly*. The ink color. The penmanship." She lifted and dropped her hands, the problem growing horns and hair and sharp, jagged teeth. "I can't very well have mismatched place cards!"

"Breathe," he instructed. She did, even though the suggestion peeved her. She was more peeved when a few deep breaths took her down a notch. "Did you know that anxiety literally shuts off the problem-solving portion of your brain? You need that part, Rye. So. Who do you know that does calligraphy?"

"No one," she answered automatically. "Wait. My mom."

"*Your mom*? How could you forget something like that?" He chuckled.

"I didn't forget. It's one of her hobbies. Along with painting landscapes, making mosaics from broken dishes and quilling."

"What the fuck's quilling?"

"It's where you roll these little strips of paper into flowers or—you know what? Never mind. The point is my mom has a lot of artsy hobbies. She doesn't do any of them for a living."

"Do you have samples of the calligrapher's penmanship? Can your mom copy it?"

"Maybe." Rylee's heart buoyed. Could the fix be this simple?

"Do they live close by?"

"They do. My hometown is about forty-five minutes away from here. If she's willing to do this for me, I could drive there and be back by this afternoon." Which gave Rylee plenty of time to check on the preparations for the rehearsal dinner and greet Ari and Ex when they arrive. "Let me make a quick phone call."

Her mother was home, and not only was she willing to help with the place cards, she was also excited to try her hand at it. Rylee gathered the box of place cards that were already done, plenty of extra card stock, and headed for the door. As she turned to ask Trick if he needed the office key in her absence, she found him gathering his camera bag.

"Where are you going?"

"I'm coming with you."

"What do you mean you're coming with me?"

"This is behind-the-scenes gold. I'm not letting an opportunity to film last-minute place cards and your mom as the emergency ringer pass us by. You painted this like a Greek tragedy two minutes ago. This is the big save."

"I overreact sometimes," she mumbled, slightly embarrassed for leaping off the deep end when the answer had been right in front of her face. If Trick hadn't been here, she didn't know if it would have ever occurred to her to call her mother and ask for help.

"It's what makes you good at what you do." He took them the long way through the TCC, grabbing a few bottles of water from a cooler on the way. She stopped him before he asked the kitchen staff to whip up a charcuterie board for the road.

"Want me to drive?" he asked as she unlocked her mother's Mercedes.

"No. You film. I'll drive. It'll give me something to do besides watch the minutes tick away." In theory they would return on time for the rehearsal dinner. Barring any unforeseen circumstances that would cause a delay. This wedding had been chock-full of unforeseen circumstances. While she didn't want to jinx herself, she was aware anything could happen. The passenger in her car was all the proof she needed.

"Will your dad be there, too?" Trick asked once they were on the road.

"Possibly. He works from home more often than not these days. He has stepped back some from his position as CFO."

"Certified… Frisbee Overseer?" Trick laughed at his own corny joke. "What's his business?"

"Baird Textiles. My great-grandmother's company originally. Baird was her maiden name. She handed down the company to my dad and his brother, who is the CEO."

"Ah yes, Chief Elephant Operator."

She couldn't help chuckling. "Close. Baird provides luxury fabrics for some of the top industries in the world. Hotels, theaters, awards shows."

"*The* red carpet?"

"Rumor has it." She hadn't been fascinated with her father's business when she was younger, not until she'd started planning weddings and had recognized Baird fabrics seemingly everywhere she went. The more upscale venues were outfitted with Baird drapes, carpeting and even artwork. She hadn't been able to keep from feeling a surge of pride. "I'll introduce you as the videographer when we arrive to avoid any impolite questions."

She could practically hear her mother now. *"Who is this man you've brought home to us, Rye? How did you meet him? What is his family like? Do they have ties to Royal?"*

Her mother, and father for that matter, had always had their sights set on a wealthy beau for Rylee. Until she and Louis had split, she hadn't seen their meddling for what it was. Not quite an arranged marriage, but possibly its cousin.

"I'm not a videographer." She glanced over to find Trick's mouth screwed into a curve of displeasure. "No offense to the people who are videographers."

"If I say filmmaker, they'll ask you what you're famous for," she warned.

"So tell them the truth. Or are you embarrassed to be seen with a lowly social media content creator?"

"*The truth* is that you were famous for wedding crashing and I've been thwarting your advances and preparing for your invasion for months."

"Invasion?" He laughed as he took hold of her free hand. "You didn't thwart me for long. I woke up in your bed this morning, and I'm planning on being in it tonight."

"None of which I care to share with my parents."

"That's fair." He kissed her hand and dropped their linked fingers onto his leg. "Videographer it is."

"Social media superstar," she corrected herself. "Can I leave out the wedding crashing part?"

Fourteen

Trick had shot some footage out the window of the car, but let Rylee know he'd shut off the camera before revealing her parents' house number. She turned into a ritzy neighborhood, each house larger than the last. She navigated a few more streets before they arrived in a cul-de-sac, with a single house on a hill sitting behind a row of trees. He realized when she turned into the driveway that the mansion was their destination.

"Holy shit. You grew up here?"

"I did." She parked in the cobblestone driveway in front of a garage with four extra-wide doors. He had grown up in a nice house in a well-to-do neighborhood, but Rylee's family home was next-level.

They stepped out of the car at the same time two men holding golf clubs strolled into the grass. One was older. One younger. Trick started for the house but soon realized Rylee wasn't next to him.

"What's up, Peaches?"

"That's my dad. And Louis."

"Louis. As in your ex, Louis?"

"Yes. I have no idea why he's here." The older of the two men raised a hand to wave, while her ex-fiancé grimaced as he tugged on a leather glove.

Trick felt the instant pull to protect her, but Rylee had already stepped around him.

"Louis. This is a surprise." She smiled genially, which Trick saw as unnecessary. Then she kissed her father on the cheek. "Hi, Daddy."

Trick sized up her ex in spite of himself. Louis was tall and lanky, with hard eyes and a short, neat haircut. He wore a collared polo shirt tucked into his trousers. Everything about him screamed *boring*.

"Your mother mentioned you'd be stopping

by," her dad said. "I thought you were the one at the door, but I found Louis on the porch instead."

"New golf grips," Louis said in explanation, raising the club in his hands and giving Trick an assessing look. Rylee, born and bred into this kind of bullshit disguised as politeness, didn't miss the awkward pause and was quick to fill the silence.

"This is Trick MacArthur. He's shooting video for the wedding I'm planning. He tagged along to film some footage."

Trick tried not to visibly react to the phrase "tagged along." It was clear from the way Louis looked down his nose that he'd already labeled Trick as an underling.

"Trick?" Her father's face scrunched.

"Short for Patrick," Rylee said. "Trick, this is my father, Meyer, and his coworker, Louis. We grew up together."

"We did more than that," Louis grumbled, earning a look of disapproval from Meyer Meadows and a matching one from his daughter. What a dick. "How long have you been a videographer, Patrick?"

"He's a filmmaker, actually," Rylee interjected. "He has one of the largest channels on social media in the world."

"Oh?" Louis asked, his tone flat. "What's your niche?"

"Weddings!" Rylee said. "If you'll excuse us, we are on a time-crunch. Is Mom in her office?"

"Or in the kitchen, fussing over hors d'oeuvres," Meyer answered before he stepped onto the green front lawn and took a swing with the club in his hand. "You'll have to give me the number of your pro shop," he was saying to Louis. "If new grips shave three strokes off my game, I'll finally make par."

Whatever the fuck that meant. Trick offered a tight nod as he passed by Louis, refusing to make small talk. He already didn't like the guy for what he'd put Rylee through, before dumping her, no less. That her father still employed him was infuriating. No wonder Rylee moved to LA.

"Do you play golf?" Trick asked her as they entered the house.

"I used to. I rarely find the time now." She angled through the foyer, past a sitting room and through a corridor leading to the kitchen.

The house was palatial, their footsteps echoing off the marble flooring as they made their way through it. Evidence of the Meadows' wealth showed in every tapestry, fussy vase and haughty design choice. Opulence had its place, but this house, for all of its space, was stuffy.

They approached an older woman who was cleaning off a countertop in the kitchen.

"Hi, Abigayle. Have you seen my mother?"

"In her office. I sent Anya up with a tray of macarons and a pitcher of lemonade."

"Perfect. Thank you." Rylee left the kitchen and led Trick up a set of stairs. They passed Anya on the way, a woman around their age who Rylee hugged mid-staircase. In a long hallway upstairs, Rylee and Trick entered the third room on the left.

The office was every bit as large as the kitchen, and had not one but two balconies complete with French doors. Rylee's mother was standing at a side table, pouring lemonade into glasses. Her eyebrows shot up when she saw Trick. "I assumed when Anya brought three glasses that Louis would be joining us. That doesn't make sense now that

I think about it, since he never cared for your hobbies."

Rylee's smile stayed plastered on, but Trick could tell she hadn't enjoyed hearing the career she'd built from scratch being referred to as a "hobby."

"Hello. I'm Regina."

"Trick MacArthur." Shifting his handheld tripod and camera into his left hand, he shook Rylee's mother's hand with his right.

"Patrick," Rylee inserted, and for some reason that bugged him. "He's filming behind the scenes for Ariana and Xavier's wedding and you are about to have a starring role."

"Oh, dear. I should have had my makeup done." Regina fluffed her hair, light blond like her daughter's, but longer. She was wearing a pantsuit with large rhinestones on the sleeves and a pair of shoes that added a few inches to her smaller stature. It was no secret where Rylee had inherited her height. Meyer was a good foot taller than his wife. Trick wondered if it'd been Regina who had insisted Rylee wear high heels with everything.

"Let's go over what I need, and you can

practice mimicking the calligrapher's style. Once you're comfortable, if you wouldn't mind Trick, erm, Patrick filming you while you write, that would be great. Of course, he doesn't have to show your face if you want to remain anonymous."

"Don't be silly." Regina had already pulled out a compact and was generously applying lipstick. "Patrick, you'll only film me in the best light, correct?"

"You have my word," he assured her.

After her mother and Trick were comfortable in each other's presence, Rylee excused herself to take a phone call. This one was from Colin, who asked if there were any additional guests expected at tonight's rehearsal dinner. He and his team were doing the cooking for the event. He'd assured her he had plenty of food, but preferred to quadruple-check the headcount.

"I appreciate that quality in you, Colin," she told him as she stepped outside.

"Tell Corynna that." His Irish accent was dreamy, but took on a sensual quality whenever he mentioned the woman who'd once been his enemy and was now the love of his life.

Rylee thanked him for checking in and promised to see him tonight. Her father, looking like a gender-swap of her with his own cellphone pressed to his ear, nodded as he bypassed her and went inside. Work took precedence with him. Not for the first time, she recognized that quality in herself. One that Louis, who regarded her with a frown as he tucked his club back into its bag, had always been quick to point out.

"You look good." His eyes roamed over her hair as if deciding if he liked her updated cut. "Not as professional as you could be. That dress is a little short."

She chuffed her disagreement, but her hand automatically smoothed over the material. "Are you finished showing off your clubs?"

"Nearly. Your father's coming out with me to play nine after his call." Louis tucked his hands into his pockets. "I have a few minutes to talk."

She didn't have anything to say to him, but she supposed chatting about the weather or work was innocuous. “How are things at Baird?”

“Good. The same.”

“That’s good. How are your parents?”

“They’re fine. Are you planning on telling me why you’re hanging around with the internet’s most infamous wedding crasher?”

She blinked, shocked that Louis had recognized Trick. Maybe she should have omitted his last name from the introduction. Or made one up.

“You’re wondering how I knew, aren’t you?” He glanced around her parents’ estate. “People at work have been talking about the video you were in with him. You fell off a ladder. He caught you. Ridiculous stunt.”

“It wasn’t a stunt,” she found herself defending.

“You hanging out with him sure as hell is. A content creator, Rylee?” He shook his head the way he’d done whenever he’d been disappointed with her. “A bit below your pay grade, isn’t he?”

“We’re…friends.” Not that it was any of Louis’s business, but he had made a lot of assumptions and she didn’t care for it one bit.

"You mean like we're friends?" He leaned casually on the railing, never taking his eyes off her. She used to think his blue-gray irises were attractive, but now the color appeared cold. "Forgive me for saying so, but someone should."

"Louis—"

"I can't believe this is the life you've chosen. We had a future planned, Rye. One where I would make enough money for both of us so you wouldn't have to stoop to do people's bidding. My God, you've even roped your mother into handwriting place cards for a talentless celebrity couple."

"They're not talentless."

"It's demeaning."

"No, it's not. She was happy to help."

He shook his head. "I'm insulted. I could've given you anything you wanted and you chose to be a servant. Why do you cater to rich people when you are one yourself? Explain that to me."

"Why do you choose to work for my father instead of start your own business?" she shot back. "Isn't that beneath you?"

He laughed in that condescending way he'd

perfected. “Nice try, but no, a three-generation multimillion-dollar corporation is a far cry from you scuttling around counting chairs for guests. When you were with me, did you ever consider the chair you were sitting on?

“Of course you didn’t. You were with me. You were taken care of. Anything you needed, wanted, dreamed of having, I provided. I know you’ve been under a lot of stress with this wedding. Your father mentioned it while we were out here chipping balls.”

Well. That was the last time she shared her job stress with her mother. She hadn’t thought it’d be relayed to Louis via her father.

“He’s worried about you. He wanted more for you too, Rye. He wanted me for you.”

“He wasn’t the one who would have had to marry you,” she snapped. “Let’s not forget that you were the one who left, Louis.” Her voice crept up an octave. “You were the runaway groom, remember?”

“No need for theatrics.” Louis had perfected being infuriatingly calm. He waved a hand in the general direction of the house. “Once this boy is out of your system, you should reconsider the life you left behind. It's not too late for us to try again."

She didn't know which argument to make first. "We split up three years ago."

"Which gave you time to grow up. You tried out a business, you gave living in California a shot, and now you know how many people are willing to take advantage of you." He smoothed a lock of hair away from her face. "Make no mistake, Rye. Trick is using you. He has no intention of sticking around and being the man you need. He doesn't have a real job. He can't provide for you like I can."

When he brushed her cheek with his knuckles, she smacked his hand away. Her throat was full of words to say, but she had too much tact to say half of them. She wanted to inform her buffoon of an ex that she and Trick were having incredible sex, and that he'd taught her things about her body Louis never bothered to learn. Then again Louis might tell her father she said that, which would be horrific on several levels.

Maybe she would point out that there was more to Trick than his online antics, and that his dreams and goals were worthy of pursuit. But before she could arrange any one of those phrases into spoken form, the door swung aside and her father stepped out of it, his bag of clubs on his shoulder.

"Your mother is asking for you. Ready to hit the links, Louis?"

"We're almost done here." She propped her hands onto her hips and faced her ex. "I don't need you to provide for me. I can provide for myself. You are not, and will never be, a consideration. Not ever again."

"Rylee," her father barked.

"You can go now," she shooed Louis toward the steps. "Have fun, Daddy. As much as you can have with him."

Louis's upper lip curled.

"Erm, I'll drive." Her father started for the garage.

Louis shouldered his golf bag. Before he stepped off the porch, he offered a parting jab, "You're better than this. You know it, I know it. *Trick* knows it, too. You know where to find me."

She sure did, she thought as he walked away. Right up her father's ass.

Fifteen

Trick had never seen Rylee so infuriated, which was saying something as his mere presence in Texas had pissed her *way* off at first. Outside of her parents' house, he found her sitting on the white porch swing, pushing herself back and forth. Her hair lifted in the breeze created by the overhead fans. He'd thought at first that her cheeks were red because of the heat, but then he followed her gaze to the retreating car holding her ex-fiancé and her father.

Trick sat next to her on the swing. She didn't take her eyes off the long driveway even though her father's car was long gone.

She seemed to notice Trick's presence belatedly.

"All set?" she asked, her smile tired.

"Your mom said it'll take a few minutes for the ink to dry. I'm no professional, but I think she did a great job. She's a perfectionist so it had to be just right. She reminds me of you."

Rylee turned her head. "You sound surprised."

"I am, actually." When Rylee had described how she'd been raised, he'd assumed the women in her family were robotic servants with the men their controllers. "Pleasantly."

A beat of silence passed. They continued swinging, their feet pushing against the boards. Trick decided to take a wild stab at what was bothering her. "Louis said something stupid, I take it."

She grunted. "Lots of stupid things. Including telling me that I was welcome to come back to him when I'm done being rebellious."

"He sees your business as a rebellion?"

"And you."

He had to laugh, which drew a genuine smile from her. That was good to see. "Men like him have no confidence. It's an act. He's trying to sound big while being small. He isn't aware that you can see through him because he can't admit to himself that you're smarter than he is."

She kissed Trick so fast he never saw it coming. Once her lips pressed against his, though, he responded. Cupping the back of her neck, he deepened the kiss, tilting his head to further drink her in. She tasted like sunshine and capability. Like a woman who would never trade her career for a paltry offering made by an insecure man-baby.

Trick admired Rylee all the way down to those uncomfortable shoes she wore. The more he thought about how much she didn't like them, the more irked he became. As she discovered more about herself, he hoped that she would let go of anything and everything that didn't serve her. Men and shoes in particular. He also hoped that he wasn't part of what she cast off, even as he acknowledged that he didn't want to explore that thought too deeply.

He tried to stop kissing her, honest to God, but the moment her tongue touched his, he forgot why. He set his equipment on the swing to free his other hand. Now he could cup both sides of her face. *Perfect.*

If she was using him as a way to release her pent-up emotions, he would gladly give her what she needed. She'd become a safe place for him as well, an uncommon occurrence in his world. When she'd brought up a one-night thing this morning, he'd been offended. Strange, considering he'd never before argued with a woman about keeping things light.

Rylee was different from any other woman he'd known. They naturally melded together. Spending time bouncing ideas off of each other was easy, and fun. He didn't know how to define what was happening between them, but he knew what they were doing was the *opposite* of a one-night stand.

Lips tingling, he surfaced from her mouth at the same moment he heard the delicate clearing of a throat behind them.

Rylee unwound his arms from her body and jerked away. He instinctively knew they hadn't been interrupted by one of the house staff. When he turned his head to look over his shoulder, Rylee's mother was standing in the doorway, a small flat box in her hands.

* * *

"Sorry to interrupt." Her mother's voice held a note of amusement disguised as a singsong lilt.

While Rylee wouldn't have expected her to be clutching her pearls, she had expected Regina Meadows to offer censure for what she'd witnessed.

"I have your place cards ready. Trick agreed that I matched the handwriting of the originals quite closely."

"You have talent, Regina," he said with warm familiarity. What had those two talked about upstairs while Rylee had been listening to Louis be a butthead? She had expected her mom to be cordial to Trick, but she hadn't anticipated them chatting.

Rylee had never brought home a boyfriend her parents didn't know. Trick, as it turned out, was the first man in her life that had required an introduction.

"Thank you, Trick. I pride myself on my penmanship, so that means a lot." Her mother's mouth twisted. "I suppose your father and Louis are on the golf course. I do not know why he continues to be loyal to the man who broke your heart."

"Louis didn't break my heart, Mom" Rylee was quick to argue. "He broke our engagement."

"You don't have to downplay it, darling."

"I'm not. I didn't love Louis in the way a wife should love a husband." Rylee frowned. This wasn't an epiphany she'd had before, and she wasn't entirely sure where it had come from. It sure as hell felt true, so she continued with her stream of thought. "I don't know if I dated him because he was convenient or because I was shuffling along a chosen path."

"Ultimately, you un-chose that path." Her mother sounded almost defensive before she added, "I'm proud of you for speaking your mind. Your father and I were less than thrilled to hear that the wedding was called off, but only because we assumed you were happy. Then you started your business and we saw what happy actually looks like on you."

"Thanks," Rylee said, meaning it.

"Does she seem happy to you, Trick?"

To his credit, he didn't shift under Regina's scrutiny. "She does."

Rylee puffed her chest. Trick had seen the real her. Not as a perfectionist who worried herself ragged over every detail, but as a strong woman who knew her own mind. How many times had he poked fun at her for wearing shoes she hated? Like he'd been daring her to kick them and go barefoot. Too many to count.

"Try not to take your father's behavior personally. You know he'll golf with anyone." When her mother's comment failed to lighten the mood, she added, "For all of Louis's faults, he *is* a good employee. Not CEO material, though. Despite what he thinks, he will never be in charge."

"I suppose that stick in his ass comes in handy. You can prop him in the corner during long meetings," Trick said.

Regina, her hand on her chest, let out an unladylike guffaw. Rylee wasn't sure what was funnier—Trick's quip or her mother losing her composure.

"Trick, you must come back and visit." Regina handed the box of place cards to Rylee. "Bring him for dinner the next time you're both in town."

Rylee swallowed the argument that bringing him to dinner wouldn't be possible. This was a four-night stand, not a relationship. But her mother didn't need to know the gory details. She stood from the porch swing. "We should be going. Thank you for this. You're a lifesaver."

"You're welcome. It was fun to be a part of a couple's special day. Trick, I enjoyed talking with you."

"I enjoyed it as well." He kissed her mother's cheek and then he and Rylee stepped off the porch and angled toward the driveway.

Before they got too far, Regina called out, "If you ever need a calligrapher in the future, feel free to consider me!"

Trick's eyebrows sprang to his forehead when he exchanged glances with Rylee, who offered a clumsy, "Oh-okay. Sure," in answer to her mother's offer.

Sixteen

Ariana and Xavier were due to arrive at Sheen well after the seven o'clock rehearsal dinner, so Rylee was at ease as she glided through the restaurant and into the kitchen where Colin was bustling about with his staff. He finished instructing one of his sous-chefs before dashing over to her, his eyes wild.

"Last minute change-up, Rylee," he said, his Irish brogue thicker than usual. Maybe stress amplified his accent. "The dinner is now a cocktail party, so we've reimagined the menu."

"A…cocktail party?"

Colin went on to describe the small plates

he'd whipped up last minute, developed from ingredients that were originally going to make up a five-course dinner.

"Xavier called right after I talked to you. He said Ari wanted a casual cocktail party with tapas, and that they extended invitations to out-of-town guests." He stroked his beard as he studied Rylee with his penetrating green stare. "He didn't call you?"

"Um. I, uh, must have missed a text." She slapped on a smile.

"Well, it shouldn't change anything for you. Corynna's setting up the flowers now. If you see her, can you send her back?" His sous chef called out and Colin answered succinctly before swiping his brow. "It's a bloody madhouse."

"Is there a message I can pass along to her to save you a few seconds?" The kitchen was literally vibrating with activity. "You seem to have your hands full."

"Yes." He gave her a handsome smile. "Tell her I need the edible flowers for the gorgonzola and fruit plate. Thank you."

"You're welcome."

Rylee left the kitchen projecting much more

ease than she felt. Another last-minute change from the bride and groom? She hoped there weren't any more surprises to come in the next few days.

She checked her texts, but didn't see one from Ari or Ex. Odd. Then she noticed she had zero texts. *Then* she noticed the little airplane symbol in the corner of her screen. Her phone was on airplane mode? Panicked that she'd missed more messages than she cared to acknowledge, she turned off airplane mode and waited for the flood. Three texts came through, and her email showed ten unread messages. Not great, but not a disaster.

Ari's text to Rylee read, "We are switching up the menu for tonight but Ex called Colin personally. See you at Sheen!"

Rylee's heart was leaping out of her chest, unspent adrenaline zipping around her bloodstream. She pursed her lips and blew out a breath. While tonight was an upset she hadn't seen coming, everything seemed to be under control. Shoulders back, she replied to Ari and scanned the other incoming messages to make sure there were no more emergencies to head off.

Over the next hour, guests poured into the private seating area in the rear of Sheen, more than the originally planned-upon bridal party, but still a reasonable number. Rylee greeted everyone with a smile, and a few friends with hugs, including Dionna who had come directly to her.

"You are exquisite." Dee held Rylee's hands out to her sides and admired her coral dress.

It was fitted, cocktail-length, and had a decorative bow on the shoulder that normally would have been a bit much for her. But it had seemed the right vibe for a rehearsal dinner…even one that had turned into an hors d'oeuvres and cocktail party.

Dee cocked her head. "What's different?"

"Um. Nothing?"

"Your hair is down. Your dress is brightly colored." Dee's eyes popped wide. "You slept with that hunk of yummy wedding crasher, didn't you?"

Rylee shushed Dee, but the other woman did not oblige.

"I knew it!" Dee hugged Rylee, saying into her ear, "Your secret is safe with me."

Once that mini interrogation was done,

Rylee found Corynna, who appeared half as harried as Colin. She relayed the message from the chef, and Corynna hustled outside to gather the edible flowers she'd brought over from her shop.

Rylee wasn't quite in Relax Mode yet, though. As more guests arrived, she had to slip out of the private area to alert Sheen's staff that they needed more chairs, and at least one more table. Both were delivered quietly and efficiently, and with as little disruption as possible.

The waitstaff, dressed in black, served wine and champagne as well as some sort of puff pastry that looked amazing. Her mouth watered at the thought of a nibble of one of Colin's last-minute creations, but she didn't want to take food from the guests. Best to wait and make sure everyone was fed first.

A warm hand slipped around her back and gently tugged her close. She knew it was Trick without turning. Not only because of the faint scent of his cologne, but also because she'd come to know his touch. Gentle but firm. In a few short days, he'd become so familiar to her.

She relaxed against him, realizing that she'd been holding tension in her shoulders for the last few hours.

"Welcome to the rehearsal cocktail party," she said to Trick as she waved to Sasha, Ari's sister, who was on the other side of the room.

"No dinner? I'm starving." He held up his cellphone and angled the camera at them, never taking his hand off Rylee's back. "Smile pretty, Peaches. We're going live."

Before she could protest, he hit the red button and gave the camera a wide grin. "Hey, Tricksters," he greeted his fan club. "I'm here with the beautiful, beguiling Rylee Meadows, resident wedding planner and savior of celebrity nuptials. You asked for more, and here she is." He faced her, his jovial smile going a long way to soothing her nerves. "You look stunning. Who are you wearing?"

She laughed at his shtick. The way his eyes twinkled when he looked her up and down hinted that he liked what he saw.

"This is one of Keely Tucker's earlier designs. You might recognize it. Didn't you leak some of her stuff to the public at one point?"

"And she's feisty," he said, never taking his

eyes off hers. "I'm going to shake a few trees and find out what Ari and Ex's guests think of Sheen and Colin Reynolds's culinary creations." He removed his hand and tilted his head. "I'll find you later, Peaches."

That rumbled promise left a trail of tingles down her arms. She watched as he made his way across the room, stopping to say hello to Dee and Tripp first.

With a spring in her step that wasn't there before Patrick had come over to say hello, Rylee walked over to greet a pair of new arrivals.

Trick thanked Dee and Tripp for their time and shut off the camera. One of his series on his social media channel was a three-question interview with the guests. Typically he saved it for the reception, but as he wouldn't be filming any of the wedding or reception, he'd been forced to be creative.

He cast a glance over at Rylee, who couldn't look hotter unless she were holding the tray of flaming baked Alaska that was being whisked across the dining room of the restaurant. She was also calmer than usual. Oh, sure, she was hiding stress beneath a stunning smile, but he could tell she was no longer fretting over the party.

She lifted her foot and adjusted a strap on her gold high-heeled shoe, grimacing the entire time. He shook his head, and then had an idea…

His phone buzzed in his hand with an incoming text. Then another. Then one more. "What the…?"

Todd, via group text was the first. Yo, Trick! We're in Royallllll.

Yee-haw! came Rusty's reply to all.

James chimed in with a gif of a cowboy riding a Mustang into the sunset.

We're staying in a fancy-ass hotel called the Bellamy. Planning on crashing the Noble-Ramos wedding. Let us know when to sync up.

Following Todd's text was a photo of the three of them—more acquaintances than friends now that they no longer ran a social media channel together. Trick hadn't hung out with his buddies in at least a year. Why had they crawled out of the woodwork to fly to Royal?

Not sure on timing yet. Beer tomorrow,

Trick texted back. He looked over his shoulder at Rylee. He couldn't very well explain to his friends that there would be no crashing via text message. He'd have to tell them in person.

On his channel, he'd maintained that he was filming the pregame, but he hadn't let his fandom know that he would not be sharing any of the Noble-Ramos wedding or reception. Frankly, he hadn't decided if he would or not. He was filming an interview with Ari and Ex tomorrow. There was an outside chance of gaining their blessing to shoot footage of their big day. Asking for permission was weird, but not in a bad way. Trick was looking forward to showing up invited rather than crashing an event where he didn't belong.

Tonight! Rusty argued via text.

Shots, baby! James replied.

Shit to do, Trick answered the group, but he had to smile. As boneheaded as they could be, they were good guys. He hadn't shared that he was radically changing his public content, so it wasn't their fault they didn't know. He texted over the address of a cantina in town and suggested that his buddies grab dinner and drinks there *without* him.

A few texts followed with middle-finger emojis and good-natured razzing. Trick ignored them. Tomorrow, he'd straighten it out and let them know what was up.

Applause filled the room and Trick looked up to see Ari and Ex walk in. Looking every inch the celebrity in a skin-tight pale gold gown, Ari waved. Ex was in a suit and tie, sans jacket. He took a bow which elicited more applause and laughter from friends and family.

Rylee materialized at Ari's side and directed them to a table that had been reserved for the bride and groom. She then attempted to fade into the background.

For Trick, she hadn't faded a bit. Or maybe it was that she *couldn't* fade. Wherever he was with her, Rylee glowed like the north star, far outshining the wealthy entrepreneurs in their midst.

He knew why he was looking forward to showing up invited to this wedding. Because Rylee had been the woman to invite him. She was the main reason he was looking forward to Saturday.

Maybe the only reason.

Seventeen

Rylee was exhausted. Her feet ached. A tension headache was forming between her eyes. She was tired of smiling. She was starving. She wanted nothing more than to go back to her room, finish eating the box of chocolates and then collapse on her bed and sleep for twelve hours straight.

She regarded her watch. It was nearly 11 p.m. She'd have to settle for five or six hours of sleep. *Sigh*.

She'd lost Trick at some point during the evening. He'd been filming and chatting with the guests, conducting interviews like the ones Rylee had watched on his channel before. The questions were innocent, ranging from favorite flavor of ice cream, to whether the interviewee would prefer living near the ocean or in the mountains.

She'd felt his hand on her back at least one other time during the evening and that had been when he'd handed her a plate of assorted hors d'oeuvres. He must have noticed she hadn't sampled the trays being passed around. Was there anything the man didn't notice?

Ari and Ex were making their way to the door. Rylee was glad they had thanked Colin for the last-minute arrangement. They might be particular about their preferences, and change their minds more than any couple she'd dealt with in the past, but they were also polite and kind, and never took advantage of the people helping them.

"Rylee." Ari smiled, a glimmering goddess in gold. "You were right about that wedding crasher. Everyone loved the interview questions. They thought Ex and I cooked them up."

After the happy couple had been seated at their reserved table, Rylee had informed them of Trick's plans for the rehearsal party. She'd assured them that their fans would love participating in the behind-the-scenes extras, and promised that there was nothing offside about Trick's plans. Dee happened to overhear and had backed Rylee's claim.

"Everything turned out great," Ex said now. "We'll see you and Trick tomorrow, I take it?"

"Six o'clock sharp."

"It'll have to be sharp. I want to get a good night's sleep, and we're planning on a long, hot bubble bath afterward." Ari walked her fingers up Ex's tie before kissing him. All Rylee could think about was how wonderful a bubble bath would feel right now.

She saw the couple out, waited until the last guest followed and then nearly collapsed. Not before thanking Colin and Corynna, who were in the kitchen faux arguing over which edible flowers tasted better. The kitchen staff was in cleaning mode, their pace moderately slower than earlier. Rylee said goodbye and thanked them collectively, and then left via the rear exit.

Outside, Trick was leaning against the door

of her borrowed car, his legs crossed at the ankles, tripod on the ground, his hand on the hilt. She came to a stop as her pinky toe wailed in agony. This was the first and last time she was wearing these damn shoes.

"I thought you'd gone hours ago," she said, wearily making her way to him.

"I left and then came back. I had an arrangement to make."

She regarded him with suspicion. "What kind of arrangement?"

"It has nothing to do with the wedding." He held out one hand. "Keys."

She dropped them into his palm, happy to sit on the passenger side. "I'm at your mercy."

He turned on the car. "I like how that sounds."

"Don't be too excited. I'm half asleep already." She laid her head back and shut her eyes, the entire day washing over her in one draining wave.

Two more days. Just two more days. This was crunch time, always the most challenging part of planning a wedding. But each item she ticked off the list brought her closer to the grand finale. Once the reception was winding to a close, she was home free. Then this wedding would be in the history books, another success story to add to the testimonials page of her website.

"You don't have to stay awake for where we're going. In fact, falling asleep might be considered a compliment."

He didn't give her any more hints than that. She watched out the window as he drove them back to the Bellamy Hotel. Hopefully he would tuck her in for a nap before attempting any sexual acrobatics tonight. They were running out of time to spend together, but even that ticking clock hadn't imbued her with her the *oomph* she needed.

She joked as they strolled through the lobby that she required a coffee before any of her clothes came off. He stayed quiet, holding her hand and leading her past the elevators and down another corridor.

"Where are you taking me?" She perked up when they stopped in front of a darkened window. "The spa? It's closed."

Trick leaned in, his voice low. "You said you could pick a lock, right?"

"Oh, no. No, no."

He grinned and then produced a keycard from his pocket. He swiped it and depressed the handle, holding the door open for her. “Relax, Peaches. I wouldn’t ask you to burgle the hotel spa. Come on.”

A million questions cluttered her mind as they stepped into the shadows. Manicure stations were tidy and silent, rows of nail polish lining the shelves like colorful soldiers. They passed massage rooms and a room marked “sauna” before coming to a room with a pedicure chair.

“Thank you, Janice,” Trick said to himself as he stepped into the dimly lit room. The tub at the foot of the leather chair was bubbling away, steam floating up from the basin.

“What did you do?” Rylee asked as he lowered to his knees. “What are you doing?”

“Giving you exactly what you deserve.” He unbuckled the dainty straps around her ankles and removed her uncomfortable shoes. A deep sigh worked its way up from her throat. “Have a seat.”

She sat, anticipating a pedicurist to materialize from the doorway.

“No one’s coming.” Trick slung a towel over

his shoulder. Then he sat on a short stool and lowered her feet into the water one by one. “Just me.”

“You’re—I can’t let you do this.” She started to pull her foot from the water, but he placed a hand on her knee below the hemline of her dress.

“You have to. I spent an hour here with Janice, the manager, and learned what to do.”

“How?” She couldn’t wrap her head around what was happening. Not being in a spa alone afterhours, or Trick sweet-talking the key from the manager, or the fact that he had taken one of her feet from the water and was squirting oil onto his hands. “She let you in here unsupervised?”

“Well, I had to promise we wouldn’t have sex on the massage table.”

As good as his thumb in the arch of her foot felt, she stiffened. “You didn’t.”

His grin was mischievous. “I didn’t. Relax. That’s your only job. I watched you run around and organize everything for everyone else tonight. It’s time you allowed yourself to be pampered, don’t you think?”

She eased back into the chair. He finished

massaging her foot and then traded one for the other. He poured a scoop of scented sea salt with tiny, dried roses into the tub. Slowly but surely, Rylee allowed herself to relax.

Earlier when he'd stopped in to talk to the manager of the day spa, Trick had asked if there was anyone available for a pedicure very late tonight. Janice regretfully declined, explaining that her employees were coming in early tomorrow with appointments, and that she had a family dinner tonight she couldn't miss.

Trick hadn't given up. He'd had a pampering session in mind for Rylee. He'd watched her leap hurdle after hurdle today. She'd catered to the bride and groom, who had thrown another curveball her way, and she'd handled it with the same grace and poise with which she'd handled everything else. Including him.

Rylee deserved to be spoiled.

"What if I do it?" he'd asked Janice. The manager broke into a small laugh that had crinkled her eyes at the corners. He'd gone on to explain who he was, and had shown her a few of his online videos. When he offered to mention the spa to his subscribers, he won the other woman over. She'd been looking for a unique way to advertise, and him offering to do it for free had been too good to pass up.

Janice had given him the key card and asked him to stash it in the front desk drawer when he left. She'd given him a basic rundown of how to give a woman a relaxing foot treatment, teasing that she didn't have adequate time to teach him how to polish Rylee's toes.

"I never had the chance to ask you the interview questions I asked everyone else today," he said now, digging his thumbs into the wide part of Rylee's foot. Her eyes were half-open, her body sagging on the cushy chair. "If you are coherent enough to answer them."

"You could talk me into anything right now." She moaned, a sound he felt in his groin. He reminded himself why he'd done this rather than take her back to her room. Because she'd been obligated all day today. He wasn't about to obligate her further.

"Don't tempt me," he said anyway. "Okay, question one. What is your favorite relaxing pastime? Foot massages from sexy strangers doesn't count."

She smiled, her lashes casting shadows on her full cheeks. Her lipstick had faded, her hair had gone limp and she still looked amazing. Nothing short of edible.

"You mean besides being fed chocolate in bed after being thoroughly sexed up and down?"

He groaned under his breath. There was a definite stirring below the beltline he couldn't alleviate any time soon. "Yes, besides that."

"It's boring."

"Humor me."

"I like to reorganize my pantry and spice rack."

He nearly laughed. Of course she did. But he didn't want to insult her, so he kept going. "Question two."

"Wait, what's your answer?"

"This is my interview."

Her forehead creased. "I want to know."

He'd never been asked, but he didn't have to think about his answer. "The beach, a cold beer and a sunset."

"That sounds nice." Her expression was one of longing. "I could use a vacation."

He swallowed the offer to treat her to an

evening like it. "Question two. Who is your favorite person on the planet?"

"At the moment, it's you." She gave him a wonky smile.

"Nice try." He drained the tub and dried off her feet with a towel. "It's probably hard to pick from the thousands of friends you have."

"I don't have many friends."

He laughed, assuming she was kidding.

"I'm serious. Until this wedding, where I've befriended several of the vendors, the bride and her family, I realized I don't have many friends. Any, actually. I should make some more."

"You should," he agreed, smoothing lotion onto one of her legs. He'd expected her to struggle to pick from the people who loved her.

"My mother. Is that lame?" She wrinkled her nose.

"Not lame. My answer is my sister, Cassie."

"That's sweet."

"She's great." He stopped short of telling her she'd meet his sister one day. Would she? They hadn't spoken about what would happen once they returned to their separate lives in

LA, and now didn't seem like the right time to bring it up.

"Last question. Other than water, what is the one beverage you could drink for the rest of your life?" He waited for her to say a peach Bellini. Expected it, actually. In his mind, this question was a deal breaker. He and the woman he was seeing could disagree on the first two questions, no problem, but the final one was nonnegotiable. There was only one practical answer.

"Coffee."

"What did you say?" He paused mid-massage with his hands on her calf, his pulse quickening.

"Coffee. It's the possible answer. What about you?"

He stood, offering his hand to help her up. "Same exact answer."

On her feet, she gazed into his eyes. "Thank you for this."

"You're welcome." They both looked over at her discarded shoes. "Want me to carry you to your room?"

Laughter shook her shoulders. The tension in her body was a memory. He'd wanted to treat her, and she'd let him. He'd come here with the most noble of intentions, but now that she was looking at him with a twinkle in her eye and those dimples were on display, well, hell. How could he keep from wanting her?

"You don't have to carry me there." She wedged her feet into her shoes, but she didn't release his hand. Squeezing his fingers in hers, she said, "But you should join me."

Eighteen

The second she stepped from the elevator, Trick wrapped his free arm around her waist and gave her a hard kiss. Their tongues tangled as they stumbled in the direction of her suite. She didn't take her mouth from his as she blindly fished her key card from her purse. Or maybe she couldn't.

Warmth slid through her veins as he made out with her. His lips were firm and unyielding, like the firm erection pressed against her. Her pulse sped, her nipples tightened. She nearly forgot where she was—in the hallway of the elite and luxury Bellamy Hotel. Had she ever been so turned that she didn't care where she was or if someone caught her?

Easy answer. *No.*

Trick seemed equally overcome as they half tripped, half walked down the corridor. She smiled against his smile but the levity died quickly when they reached her suite. After she made three clumsy attempts to insert the key card, he took it from her and successfully disengaged the lock. They spilled into the room, him pausing to set aside his gear and her purse on the desk before steering them to the bed. He stopped kissing her long enough to hang the do not disturb sign on the door handle.

She kicked off her shoes and he rushed toward her. He wasn't smiling now. She preferred the intense version of him. The man who couldn't wait to strip her naked and put his lips on her body. She'd appreciated the version of him downstairs, too. The man who'd gone the extra mile to treat her.

He had a reputation for being a nuisance and a bad boy, but she'd seen a different side of him. Patrick "Trick" MacArthur had more tricks up his sleeve than showing up where he wasn't invited.

Illustrating one of them now, he shimmied her dress up and over her hips, bunching it at her waist. He flattened his palm and slipped it into her panties, stroking her folds with the tips of his fingers. She'd been slick the second his tongue had touched hers. It was like her body had known what was coming and had readied her for his exploration.

She reached behind her and unzipped the top of her dress, pulled it over her head and tossed it aside. Inside-out, no less. A fleeting thought about how it would be unforgivably wrinkled and require prompt dry cleaning vanished when he set his lips over the lace of her bra. He suckled her nipple through the fabric, leaving it damp and warm, as he stroked her below. He complemented each stroke with his thumb on her clit. By the time he lightly grazed her nipple with his teeth, she was shuddering.

The orgasm rushed over her like a tidal wave, clearing her mind of her to-do list, her schedule, and the worry over how much sleep she'd lose tonight. There was only the feeling of sparks dancing on each of her erogenous zones.

"Goddamn." He kissed her mouth—or tried, anyway. She could barely muster the strength to pucker. His voice was rough and raw when he complimented her. "That was the most beautiful thing I've ever watched. Do you have any idea how gorgeous you are when you come?"

Her hands in his hair, she played with the longer strands. "I love your hair." She kissed him. "I love your mouth." She kissed him again. "I love your fingers."

"Thanks, Peaches." His voice was strained. Perhaps because she'd rerouted her hand to his cock and was stroking him through the fabric of his pants.

"I want you. Right now. Before I come down from this incredible high. You're so hot."

He laughed, a low raspy sound. "Okay, okay. You don't have to convince me."

He shoved her hand aside and slipped out of his pants. A moment later she was steered toward the bed and pushed down onto it. He joined her, unhooking her bra and setting his mouth to her breasts. She was hovering in a hazy, gauzy post-sex veil. That was new for her. That probably meant something. Not that she had the energy to sort through it now. There would be time to think later. Right now all she wanted to do was feel.

Chest to chest, he placed a kiss on her throat and whispered into her ear. "Give me those blue eyes, Peaches."

Lazily, she gazed up at him. Her vision was filled with dark hair and piercing hazel eyes. After watching his videos, she'd admitted to herself that he was handsome. What she saw now far surpassed that. He'd become more. Without her permission and without her realizing it.

"I want to watch your face this time, too." He tilted his hips and slid past her folds. Once he was nestled deep inside of her, he paused to allow both of them to appreciate the snug fit.

She couldn't stop staring. He made no effort to look away. It was like they were each witnessing something neither of them had expected.

"Ready?" he asked, his voice hoarse.

She nodded and he began to move. He thrust into her, his gaze locked with hers, his arms tight around her. He heeded her request for "harder, faster" as another orgasm galloped to the drumbeat of her heart.

She shouted her release, losing herself in the vivid colors that sprang to life on the backs of her eyelids. Holding on tight, she soaked in every bit of what he gave her. She felt dampness from his brow when he dropped his head onto her chest. And pressure when he came inside her, his hips pumping helplessly as he finished.

His back muscles had tightened and she hugged him close, holding him together after she'd flown apart. A heated breath coasted along her neck followed by one word. "Fuck."

"I love that part of you the best." Her voice was a froggy croak. She needed water. She needed sleep. She needed another orgasm. Hell, maybe two.

Or maybe a lifetime of them.

"You're magical." She turned her head and kissed his ear, running her fingers through his thick hair. "Has anyone ever told you that?"

* * *

No one had ever told him he was magical.

At least, not in bed. He'd never thought of what he did between the sheets as the equivalent of making someone disappear. Though he could admit that he wasn't 100 percent present at the moment.

Each time she'd pointed out what she loved about him, his chest had caved in a bit more. Now it was dented and dinged. Another blow might shatter it completely, and then she'd find out what was inside.

What *was* inside?

He wanted to watch her come again. He wanted to whisper dirty words into her ear and watch her expression while he did it. That's why he'd wanted her to look at him. Then she did, and he'd no longer been in control, but careening out of it.

He'd been overcome. Overwhelmed. Who was this woman? He'd thought he'd known. She was the four-night stand wedding planner. Lover of peach Bellinis. Wearer of uncomfortable shoes. But Rylee had become more than a quick lay or a temporary fling.

What the fuck did *that* mean?

"You used a condom, right?" she murmured. "I seem to remember hearing a packet being torn but my brain isn't firing with all cylinders."

He had to look down to double-check, but yeah, there it was, thank Christ. "I got you, Peaches. You just lay there looking like every wet dream I've had in my life. I'll be right back."

He didn't feel as light and playful as he sounded. Though he could appreciate how hot she looked, naked on the hotel bedding, her breasts a pair of tight peaks in the room's cool air. When she tucked a hand under her cheek and batted thick, dark lashes, his heart literally skipped a beat.

Shit. He was losing it.

He offered her what he hoped was a smile before he stepped into the bathroom. He splashed his face with cold water and then eyed his dripping reflection.

"You're okay," he assured himself. "Nothing has changed. Go back out there, curl up next to her and go to sleep. When you wake up in the morning, blow her mind all over again."

He nodded. His reflection nodded back. It was a good plan. Solid. He and Rylee had two more days together. He was going to make every moment count before he never saw her again. Staying the night was the best decision. He didn't want to miss that sweet, sleepy look in her eyes first thing in the morning.

"Solid plan," he reiterated. Then he dried his face with a hand towel and opened the door.

Despite having convinced himself to stay, when he reached the bed, he heard himself tell her he couldn't. He pulled his clothes, muttering excuses about how she needed to sleep and how he'd had a long night as well. It sounded like bullshit to him, so he could only imagine how it sounded to her. Ultimately, he kissed her goodnight and left.

He refused to categorize what he'd done as running away. He simply wasn't prepared for the heavy emotions that had ridden sidecar with making love to Rylee. He didn't want to think about the future. He liked plans with an "*ish*" attached. Dinner at six-*ish*. Nightcaps at nine-*ish*. He liked surprises. He liked things up in the air. He preferred to act on instinct, whim.

Rylee wasn't that way. She was a planner. She made plans twelve, eighteen, hell, twenty-four months into the future. He'd convinced himself that he'd won her over to his way of life. *Don't think too far ahead. Go with the flow. Let it ride. Relax and enjoy.* She'd loosened up, but what if she'd also rubbed off on him?

Was he ready to be a planner?

He'd die before he turned into a rigid cyborg like her ex, Louis. That sort of pinned down, propped-up lifestyle didn't appeal. Trick didn't want to be a drone. Was that what a woman like Rylee expected? God knew her father did.

This was why he didn't have romantic relationships. They hampered his lifestyle. He couldn't make last-minute plans and do whatever he wanted when there was someone other than himself to consider.

He stepped into his dark hotel room and sat on the edge of bed, mindlessly checking the footage on his camera. Amidst the interviews of the guests tonight there were shots of Rylee. Faraway. Close-up. Sometimes she smiled, other times she looked pensive. Still others, unsure. Her smile was a bombshell that rattled his chest walls.

"Patrick MacArthur," he muttered. "What have you gotten yourself into?"

He shook his head. Not because he didn't know, but because he did. He was in deep with a woman he didn't want to walk away from. A woman he *had* to walk away from. There was only one word to describe his situation, so he said it out loud.

"*Fuck.*"

Nineteen

Rylee should've woken feeling light and happy. She should be floating through her day without a care in the world. But after Trick's hasty departure last night, she'd barely slept. Instead, she'd lain awake and thought over around and through what had happened.

Coffee in hand, she made her way to the hotel lobby, expecting to run into him and carpool over to the TCC for another busy day, but she didn't see him in the elevator or in the lobby. Or the parking lot. She hesitated, her thumb over the text message icon on her phone, before deciding not to contact him.

Last night had been amazing, life-altering. There had been a moment where an understanding had passed between them. An unspoken promise neither of them had vocalized.

Or so she'd thought.

When he'd come out of the bathroom, she'd been lying on her side waiting for him, anticipating him sliding in next to her and curling around her for the remainder of the night. She'd already begun looking forward to this morning. But he hadn't stayed.

"Peaches," he said, his smile relaxed and easy as he placed a kiss on her lips. She hummed, waiting for what came next. More chocolate in bed, maybe? "I'm heading back to my room. You're fading fast and I've already kept you up too late."

It hadn't been a question, so she hadn't answered. He'd pulled on his clothes, not appearing the least bit shaken, which was why she'd been so confused when he said goodnight and then walked out of her suite.

Odd behavior, for sure. She hadn't had a lot of experience, but after sex that good, why would he leave? Unless he was preparing to leave her permanently. Which had always been the plan, she supposed. She certainly hadn't started sleeping with her nemesis in the hopes of building a life with him.

And yet…

There was more between them than mere physical attraction. They should be able to talk about it openly. Honestly. Frustrated by her own inability to soothe herself or make a decision about where to go from here, she drove to the Texas Cattleman's Club. She parked near the side entrance, confident about her decision to show up and face Trick.

But as she entered her darkened office, her fortitude began to crumble. The way he'd run out on her last night hadn't made her feel sexy or wanted. Trick had made her feel used, just like Louis had suggested.

The wedding cake arrived at 11 a.m., delivered by a woman named Ebony and two men introduced as her "helpers." Rylee showed the trio to the kitchen where space had been cleared in the refrigerator to house the tiered cake. The two guys headed back out to the van, and Ebony and Rylee walked to her office to sign off on the safe-and-sound delivery of the cake.

"It's a masterpiece, truly," Rylee said as she scribbled her name on the invoice.

"Thank you." Ebony pushed a thick braid over one shoulder. "I wish I could be here to see Ari and Ex's reaction."

"Trust me, they're going to love it." Rylee walked Ebony to the door, chatting about the heat and how challenging it must have been to transport the cake without it melting. She'd been paying such close attention to the other woman's story about a time when the refrigeration unit stopped working in the van, that she didn't notice Trick until it was too late.

On the sidewalk, he was chatting with Ebony's helpers. Well, more than chatting. Laughing and addressing the camera while he filmed them.

"That's Trick MacArthur," Ebony said.

Rylee waited for the smile, the mention of how big of a fan Ebony was, or for her to swoon over how attractive she found him. Because who didn't? It seemed everyone he'd met worshiped at his altar.

Instead, Ebony wrinkled her nose. "I don't trust that guy."

Rylee snapped to attention. "Excuse me?"

"Sorry if you two are close. Ever since I found out he was running a hoax, I can't support what he does."

"What hoax?" Rylee's stomach clenched. What was Ebony talking about?

"The one where he pays the bride and groom to let him 'crash' the wedding. He's been spotted leaving a thick envelope full of cash money on more than one gift table. It was all over The Dallas Duchess's website."

The mention of The Dallas Duchess gave Rylee pause. It was a known gossip website, hardly the evening news, but that didn't mean there wasn't a nugget of truth to what was reported.

"On camera, he appears out of the ether, winning over guests at the reception one by one. We assume everyone falls in love with him, but in reality they've been paid off. Not even reality is real any more. It's a shame." Ebony shrugged and then gave Rylee a professional smile. "To each their own, I guess. Have fun at the wedding tomorrow."

Fun. Sure. Rylee nodded absently.

Trick finished with his camerawork, and then shook both of the other men's hands. Once the van pulled away, he strode over to Rylee. Was that a glimmer of uncertainty in his eyes, or was she imagining it?

"Morning." He was standing farther away from her than usual, which was making her suspicious. "How'd you sleep?"

"You *pay* the bride and groom to crash their wedding?"

That wasn't how she'd intended to greet him, but wasn't sure she was ready to discuss him running away from her last night. If that's what he'd done. *God.* Had she ever overthought a situation this much?

"What are you talking about?" He shot a thumb in the direction of the van driving down the road. "Is that what she told you? Where'd she hear that?"

His tone was clipped, which made her wonder if there was some truth to the accusation. "Do you?"

He ran a hand through his hair, blew out a breath and looked at the ground. Then he met her eyes and said, "How the hell did someone find out about that?"

Rylee wasn't quite fuming, but he had a feeling she would be if they'd been in the privacy of her office. Outside of the TCC, she maintained her composure. Barely.

"You let me believe that you won over the people you met at the weddings you crashed. Now you're telling me it's prearranged? You've been lying to me."

"I've never lied to you." To himself, sure. Like last night when he freaked the fuck out and left her alone in her hotel room bed. This morning he woke up feeling like a horse's ass.

He wasn't accustomed to planning for the future. His superpower was living in the moment. He'd intended to apologize to Rylee for leaving the moment he saw her. The truth was, he should have stayed and woken up with her this morning. When it came to her, he wanted to stay in the moment with her rather than panic over an unforeseen future.

But this morning he'd suffered his own bout of "cold feet" when he stepped into the elevator. Rather than go up to her floor, he pressed the button for the lobby. He'd been killing time since, shooting B footage and gathering his thoughts. It seemed he'd finally run out of time.

Her arms were folded over her breasts, one fair eyebrow raised while she waited for him to explain himself.

"The bride and groom don't know about the money." He kept his voice low. "No one does. I leave the cash anonymously, sliding it in with the other cards and gifts. I'm a wedding guest. I should bring something, right?" He offered a sheepish smile as he palmed the back of his neck, unsure how to take her blank expression.

"You're not a guest, technically."

He dropped his hand. "This isn't what you're really upset about, is it?"

Her mouth tightened. She turned on her heel and strode away from him. He followed her inside, catching the door before it shut in his face.

"Rylee. Wait. Last night—"

She spun on him, her eyes flashing a warning. "Keep your voice down."

"You're not escaping me this easily."

"Why not? I let you escape easily."

He sighed. That was fair. He gestured to her closed office door. "Please?"

She watched him for a truncated moment and then huffed her acquiescence. "Fine."

He pulled the door shut once they were inside. He wanted to kiss her, give her the apology she deserved… make love to her on the desk. Unfortunately she looked as if she might take his head off, so he decided to explain himself first.

"Last night, I left."

"No kidding."

"I shouldn't have."

Her features softened slightly. "Then why did you?"

"Because I—"

A knock at the door drew her attention.

"Don't answer that."

"I have to. This might be a fun little adventure for you to check off your bucket list, but this is my career." She pushed past him to open the door. One of the catering staff stood in the threshold saying something about a flatware shortage.

"At least nine place settings." The kid appeared to be around seventeen years old and looked like he might puke on his shoes. Probably because Rylee was shooting laser beams out of her eyeballs at him. Not the kid's fault. Trick was mostly to blame for her foul mood.

"I wonder—" she snatched a single gold fork from the kid's hand and tapped it against his nametag "—Rodney, if there is anything left that could go wrong at the last minute."

"Peaches," Trick started. It was the wrong thing to say. She aimed those laser beams at him next. He didn't flinch. "We'll fix it."

"*We* are not going to do anything. *We* are not a 'we.'" to Rodney, she said, "Is there someone else I can talk to? Someone who might have a contact at the vendor who supplies the flatware?"

"I—I don't know, ma'am." The kid sought out Trick for help, but before he could intervene, more unexpected company appeared outside of Rylee's office.

"Trickster!"

No, no. No, no, no.

Trick stepped into the corridor as his friends, Todd, James and Rusty, were barreling toward them. Todd grabbed Trick's shoulders and shook. "You owe us a beer!"

"How did they get in here?" Rylee directed that question to Trick.

"I don't know."

"You know." James nodded. Then to Rylee said, "He knows."

"I don't know." Trick shrugged off Todd's hold. "What the hell, you guys?"

"You said we were having beer. We're here for beer."

"It's barely noon," Trick said, which sent the three of them into fits of laughter.

"And to discuss our plans for Saturday," James said, not bothering to hide his intentions. Trick was supposed to meet with them today to explain that no one would be crashing the Noble-Ramos wedding. He hadn't expected them to ambush him at the TCC.

"We understand if you've been busy." Todd scanned Rylee top to bottom. "But you can't avoid us forever. We are here. We are ready to party."

"Get your *boys* out of here before I call security. On all of you." Rylee's tone was borderline lethal. She was already convinced that Trick had lied to her about paying off the brides and grooms of the weddings he crashed, and now his so-called friends were making it seem like he'd planned to include them in just that.

Rylee locked her office and clipped away from him, young Rodney at her heels.

Out of options, Trick pointed his friends to the nearest exit so he could handle at least one of his problems. "Let's go."

Twenty

After Trick and his guests had rolled out of the TCC in a plume of cologne, Rylee had followed Rodney back to his manager to discuss the flatware issue at length. The catering company had scoured their own inventory and had come up short, and the vendor they typically used for the gold cutlery hadn't been able to locate any backup sets as of yet.

Rylee was trying not to panic. A voice in her head reminded her that mismatched flatware wasn't the end of the world. Annoyingly enough, that voice sounded a lot like Trick.

He'd claimed to leave money for the couple anonymously. It irked her that she'd instantly given him the benefit of the doubt. She was trying to be mad at him, dammit. After the way he'd left last night, she should be upset. Right?

Cellphone in hand, she was tempted to contact a friend and ask her opinion. Dee came to mind. Ariana came to mind. Even Keely. New friends, but they would be honest with her. But she didn't want to burden them with her problems.

Instead she tapped in the phone number she'd secured earlier for the vendor. When a woman answered, Rylee introduced herself. She calmly explained the flatware issue, ending with a request. "If you could give me any information you have about the brand, style, and where and when you found it, I'd appreciate it."

Her friendliness had gone a long way. Rylee jotted it down the details the vendor shared onto a pad of paper on her desk. She finished the call, opened up her laptop and set her fingers to the keys. She wanted this handled by the time she met with Ariana and Xavier for their interview with Trick later. She would find the missing gold cutlery for the couple's wedding reception before they knew it'd been an issue.

The hours passed in a blink and Rylee, after several frustrating phone calls and redirects, hadn't come up with a solution. She'd even reached out to Colin Reynolds, who was using his fame and reach to contact his friends in the restaurant world. He'd struck out as well.

Shuffling along the hallway, Rylee paused to adjust her right shoe. Her pinky toe throbbed painfully, but she did her best to ignore it. A quick glance around the lounge showed no sign of Ari and Ex, or Trick.

A text from Ari pinged Rylee's phone. It read: We're at the Silver Saddle. Where are you?

Rylee responded that she was waiting for Trick in the TCC lounge, where she thought they were supposed to meet. She apologized and promised to be along shortly. Ari's "No problem!" seemed sincere, but Rylee was angry with herself for dropping the ball. It was ultimately her responsibility to double and triple-check the details to avoid miscommunication of any kind.

Halfway through typing a text to Trick,

she heard his voice. He was twenty minutes late. She assumed he'd been partying with his friends this whole time.

"What'd I tell you about those shoes, Peaches?" He stuffed his hands into his pockets, and watched her through clear, hazel eyes, which made her question her assumption.

"Ari and Ex are at the Silver Saddle waiting on us. I must have had the location wrong."

"I saw them as I was leaving the Bellamy."

"Pardon?"

"I saw them in the hotel lobby. I swung by and asked if we were meeting at the tapas bar and they said yes and told me you were waiting on me at the TCC. So, here I am." He smiled like the change of plans was no big deal.

"Why didn't you call me so I could rush over?" she practically shouted, already angling for the exit. He gently grasped her arm and swung her around to meet him, face-to-face.

"Because I also asked Ari and Ex how much time they had and they said enough that I didn't have to rush. So. I'm not rushing." He gestured to a seating area with a coffee table surrounded by a sofa and cushioned chairs. "Can we talk?"

"Now? About what?"

"About us."

Rylee sent a longing glance at the exit before deciding she could use a moment to calm down. It wouldn't be good for the bride and groom to witness her this upset. She sat on the sofa, both wanting and not wanting to address the issue that had been on her mind since she woke up this morning.

Trick sat next to her and took one of her hands in both of his. "This isn't what it started out being."

She agreed. "Which was a one-night stand."

"*Four*," he corrected with a completely captivating smile. "Four-night stand. I like you, Rylee. I think you know that."

"I like you, too."

He hesitated, stroking his thumbs over her hand.

"Well? What's the plan?"

Sure they both lived in LA, but her work took her all over the country. She assumed he traveled quite a bit too. Whose career would win if they decided to keep seeing each other?

"I don't like to talk about the future," he started, and she readied herself for a *but*. Something like *But I can't deny we have one.* What he said next was so far off she thought she'd misheard him.

"Let's not make a plan. Let's…wing it."

"Wing it?" she bit out.

"Yeah." The ease of his grin offset her tightly pursed lips.

"But you want to keep seeing me?"

"Hell yeah."

"Then we have to make a plan. Otherwise, when will we see each other? I work every weekend. What's your schedule like? How often will we be in the same state? I don't even know where your house is in LA."

"Slow down." He squeezed her hand. "Peaches, you were never part of a plan. Plans ruin everything."

Offended, she shot off the sofa. "Plans are what my life is built around. Plans are the reason you have weddings to crash. Plans are what we make with the people who are important to us."

"Plans are also chains tying you to an obligation when you'd rather be doing something else. Like right now." He stood. "I'd rather be taking you up to my hotel room or yours than interviewing the bride and groom."

"But they're the entire reason you're here!"

"They used to be. Things change. You changed everything."

Worry skittered over her bare arms like an army of ants. She wasn't sure what he was trying to say. She couldn't picture their future together, not that he'd painted one for her. He was offering her everything and nothing at the same time. How infuriating.

"Not making plans doesn't work for me."

"It might. Give it a shot." He leaned close, his lips on their way to hers. She wanted to kiss him and forget this entire stupid conversation. She wanted to relive last night. From the pampering session to the incredible sex, it'd been amazing. But if he couldn't acknowledge that they had real, concrete issues to work out—like his schedule and hers—how would they ever make it?

"It's not enough to say we'll take it as it

comes, Trick," she told him before his mouth touched hers. "I need to know what is going to happen when we both go home to LA."

"Why?" The first wrinkle of frustration appeared on his brow.

"Because I am a planner. I love planning. Planning makes me feel safe."

"Plans are not guaranteed," he pointed out. "You had plans with Louis. Those fell through. What good did your plans do then?"

"That's different."

"How?"

Because Louis had told her that he loved her. He'd proposed. They'd had an engagement party and had met with vendors and caterers and photographers. Trick couldn't bear to stay in her hotel room last night after sex, and now he thought their relationship would simply work itself out? Ludicrous.

"We don't have time for this. Ari and Ex are waiting. Like it or not, you made a commitment, Trick. One you're late for because you decided to show your out-of-town friends a spur-of-the-moment good time. But then, they're probably allergic to plans, too, aren't they?"

* * *

Rylee and Trick arrived at the Silver Saddle five minutes later. Ari and Ex were sitting at a wide round table in the corner, with what looked like one of every appetizer spread out in front of them. They offered to share, saying that the chef had given them the spread for no charge as a wedding gift.

Trick dug in, laughing and joking as if he and Rylee hadn't just argued about their future together. She watched the interaction through narrowed eyes. How was it that he got away with absolutely everything? He crashed a wedding and the guests and couple fell in love with him. He barged into town, his sights set on the Noble-Ramos wedding and their wedding planner invites him to record the festivities.

It hadn't taken much more than a peach Bellini and a smile for her invite him into her bed. He'd had Dee and Tripp, Rylee and her mother, and now Ari and Ex eating out of his hands.

He was also notoriously generous. He left envelopes full of money as wedding gifts—okay, fine, she believed he did it anonymously—changed tires for stranded couriers, and turned complete strangers into fast friends. He was confounding.

Trick set up his tripod and camera while chatting with Ari and Ex about the questions he was planning to ask them. He advised them not to worry, that this wasn't a live feed and they could yell "cut!" and start over if they needed to.

After Ari took a sip from her glass of rosé, she tilted her head. "I have to admit, Trick, we weren't sure your intentions were pure. If it hadn't been for Rylee, you'd have been kicked out of the TCC the moment we spotted you."

"Out of the great state of Texas," Xavier corrected with a smile.

"I owe a lot to her." Trick looked Rylee's way and she plastered on a smile for the sake of Ari and Ex. They didn't need to know about the drama going on behind the scenes. As far as they were concerned, there was no issue with the gold flatware or between Rylee and Trick.

"I have a question before we start." Ari leaned in. "It's been eating me up inside."

Trick mirrored her position, leaning forward as well. "I'm all ears."

"Why weddings? Why interlope on a stranger's happiest day? I don't ask out of malice, just curiosity."

Trick nodded slowly. "I know it might appear that I'm there wreaking havoc." He waved his hands in front of him to illustrate. "The truth is, I'm a romantic at heart. I'm there to capture the moments that go unnoticed. Everyone films and photographs the dancing, the cake, the bouquet toss. What about grandma crumbling her napkin in her fist as she remembers her own wedding sixty years ago? What about the first time an aunt holds her newborn niece? Lots of unexpected—" he slid his gaze to Rylee "—and *unplanned* moments happen at the wedding reception. Those are what make each wedding unique."

"That's so true." Ari, and now Ex were hanging onto Trick's every word. Rylee knew that he was speaking from the heart, which made it that much more annoying to hear. "I'm so glad we invited you to ours. Will you be catching those small moments on film?"

"I'm under strict orders not to film the wedding or the reception. Unless you override your wedding planner, my hands are tied." Trick's affable manner was boiling Rylee's blood.

"What about your friends who crash weddings with you?" Rylee snapped. "Would you like to explain to Ari and Ex why they showed up this morning, howling about how they couldn't wait to crash the wedding with you?"

Twenty-One

Rylee had been resolutely quiet since they'd sat down at the Silver Saddle, which was unlike her. Apparently, those unspoken comments had piled up, and she'd gathered enough steam to erupt.

"Is that true?" Ari asked, a worry line bisecting her brows.

"It's true," Rylee said. "Trick left with his buddies to go day-drinking and discuss your wedding. Which was why he was late meeting me, and why I was late meeting with you."

Ari blinked and exchanged a look with Ex.

"I'm sorry." Rylee shook her head, meaning it. "You trusted me to corral him. I believed he was sincere when he promised not to ruin your big day. Evidently what I say, or *plan*, means next to nothing to him." Challenge flashed in her eyes, as if she was daring Trick to speak up in front of the almost-married couple.

Challenge. *Accepted.*

"They showed up without telling me," Trick explained, keeping his eyes on Rylee. He pivoted to face Xavier and Ariana. "I don't work with them anymore. And you don't have to worry about them coming to the wedding or the reception. They showed up thinking they could jump in, since the Noble-Ramos wedding is the most trending social media topic on the planet, but I set them straight. They're on a plane to Vegas as we speak."

"Las Vegas?" Rylee's expression was pure chagrin.

"Yes, Peaches. Las Vegas." He addressed Xavier when he continued. "We were close in college. They don't know me as well now. They used to be part of my crew and we did dumb shit to gain online views and followers. They broke off to do their own thing, but used to pop in for cameos every once in a while. Until today, they didn't know my plans to go legit, or that I'm giving up crashing altogether."

"Are we your last wedding?" Ari arched an eyebrow.

"At first I was going to taper off, maybe crash one or two more, but actually…yeah. This is it for me." He blew out a breath as he digested the words he'd finally spoken out loud. He'd thought a lot about making this wedding his last, but he hadn't had the courage to admit it.

"Leaving behind the thing you're known for isn't the easiest transition to make." Ari, actress turned producer, knew of what she spoke. "The public tends to view you through one narrow lens. They rarely accept evolution."

"I know." When he moved from the good-natured prank-style videos to wedding crashing, he'd experienced an initial dip in viewership.

"If you want to grow, it's the risk you have to take," Ari said.

"I'm proud of you, baby." Ex slipped a hand around his wife-to-be's back.

"We bring out the best in each other." Ari leaned in for a kiss. Trick sneaked a peek at Rylee, who was studying her water glass as if it would tell her the future.

Future. He shook his head. That was why they were in this mess. His resistance to it and Rylee's need to plan for it. She probably wished she was clairvoyant so that there would never be any surprises. He didn't want to know how everything turned out in the end. There'd been too many pleasant surprises waiting around corners for him. Knowing the road ahead was different than anticipating the road ahead. Knowing took all the fun out of it.

"I wasn't late because I was *day-drinking* with my friends. I had an errand to run," Trick explained, needlessly at this point since Ari and Ex were gazing into each other's eyes. "I'll be attending the wedding and reception alone and invited. Unless it would make Rylee more comfortable if I skipped the event."

"Of course not." She inclined her chin proudly. She affected an expression that was as plastic as the straws poking out of their water glasses. "I'd never take that decision away from Ari and Ex. It's their big day."

He figured. What was Rylee doing if not making sure everyone else's life ran perfectly while ignoring her own preferences?

"We want you there," Ari told Trick. "And if you see any of those small, special moments that need to be captured on film, I want you to shoot them."

"I'd be honored," he answered, meaning it.

"Now that *that's* settled." Xavier said. "Let's get on with the interview."

"If you'll excuse me, I have a few last-minute preparations to handle." Rylee stood and pushed out of the high-backed chair. "I'll see you both tomorrow bright and early!"

"Thanks, Rye!" Ari gave a cheery wave, and Rylee scuttled for the exit.

Trick pretended to adjust his camera settings as he watched her. She sent one last look over her shoulder at him, and then she was gone.

Two hours later, Rylee locked the door to her private office at the TCC. She'd finalized everything there was to finalize, with one glaring exception. The gold flatware situation had not been resolved. She had gone through several stages of grief over the debacle: anger, denial, bargaining. She hadn't rounded the corner to acceptance yet. There was always tomorrow.

She was going to be out of bed at five in the morning to do research and call any potential suppliers in the area the minute they opened. She didn't have time to do that, but she wasn't about to have mismatched cutlery. Not on her watch.

As she walked to the reception area for a final once-over, she thought about Ari and Ex's interview. She hoped it had gone well. Trick was a pro, both tactful and entertaining. He also had an answer for everything. He'd had no trouble coming up with a plausible explanation as to why his rowdy friends had crashed the TCC with ulterior motives.

She'd believed him at first when he'd said they'd flown to Vegas, but over the last few hours she'd begun to have her doubts. Louis's, and even Ebony's, comments about Trick had parked themselves in the rear of Rylee's skull. She thought she'd seen a different side of Trick, but had she? What did she know about him really? For all she knew, he'd been playing the long game—his most extravagant prank yet—and was planning to crash the wedding with his bros after all.

You don't believe that.

She didn't. Not really. But she had come to another decision about the two of them.

"Hey."

Startled, she let out a shriek and spun to face the double doors she'd just walked through. Her hand on her chest, she admonished her visitor. "You scared me half to death!"

"Sorry." Trick, a box in his hands, eased the door shut behind him. He looked tired. He looked wonderful. Like the person she wanted to curl up with and fall asleep next to tonight.

"How'd it go?" She fussed with a place setting instead of looking at him, lining up the ends of the fork and the knife so that they were even.

"Great. Ari and Ex are naturals on camera. Their public will love it."

"We should stop this now," she blurted. If she didn't admit it now she never would.

"Stop what?"

"*This*. Us."

He set the box down at the guest book station, the feathery plumes blowing in the breeze created when he walked to her. "Why would we do that?"

"Because we have a fundamental disagreement about how to move forward. You don't want to make any plans. I want to make *all* of the plans."

"Again with this? What's under your need to plan everything half to death? I've admitted I'm more comfortable not knowing the future. What's your excuse?"

"You have no plan for your career! How will we know when or where *or if* we'll see each other? Are you telling me you're going to stick close to home? Because I'm not. I have a busy life. The weddings I plan take me out of town periodically."

"I'm not going to stop traveling, either but I'll be close to home for a while. As you heard me confess earlier, I'm done crashing weddings. I have hours upon hours of footage to edit and compile into content. I am so backlogged I could spend the next six months catching up."

He reached out to grip her arms. She let him. It felt good to be touched by him. To be comforted. Even when he was saying things that scared her.

"So far all we've done is argue how we should move on, not if we should move on. You want to be with me too, don't you?"

"There is no guarantee you won't show up tomorrow and pull a stunt you cooked up tonight." She shook off his hold and walked around the long table, needlessly straightening flatware as she went. "Every problem you cause can't be solved by leaving behind an envelope of money or flashing one of your charming smiles." She paused, opposite from him. "We were only supposed to last one night anyway."

He nodded so slowly it was almost imperceptible. He looked hurt, but she refused to feel guilty. He hadn't offered her anything concrete. There was nothing more to say.

"I understand that you're scared, Rylee. So am I. At least I can admit it. You know me. The real me. No one else in Royal can say that." He let out a small laugh. "Hell, not many people at home can say that. You want me to wedge myself into some tidy column because you aren't comfortable acting on impulse? Not going to happen. I couldn't follow your rules if I wanted to because every time I turn around there is a new one." He gave her his back.

"That's not true." She should have let him leave but what he'd said had etched itself into her skin, leaving her feeling raw and vulnerable. "I've been the one bending to your will, not the other way around."

"Was that so bad? The Bellinis and the kissing and the sex and the foot massage? Eating chocolate in bed?"

"Waking up alone after you walked out on me without an explanation."

"I overreacted. I owned it. But right now? This? This is you doubling down on your fears. If you stay afraid, Peaches, we'll never have a shot at more."

She wanted to scream *How much more?!* but the words wouldn't come. The truth was she *was* scared. She wanted guarantees, promises, assurances. She wanted to know that the bottom wouldn't drop out from under her if she allowed herself to get her hopes up.

"This is for you." He tapped the medium-sized cardboard box he'd carried in. "Inside is the real reason I was late to the interview. See you, Rylee."

She let him go. She didn't want to show up at the wedding and reception tomorrow with any unexplored issues between her and Trick. She had a job to do, and he'd already distracted her from doing it. She tried to blow out a sigh of relief, but the truth was she didn't feel better. Nothing had been resolved. If anything, their relationship was *un*-resolved. It had ended, but with an ellipsis.

The unmarked cardboard box he'd carried in was holding what, she had no idea. It could be a new pair of shoes—flats, she thought with a sad smile—or a nest of fake rubber snakes.

Hesitating over the closed flaps, she thought again of him asking for "more." She loved the idea of more. More friends, more weddings to plan. When it came to her romantic life, she hadn't warmed to the idea of more. The one time she'd reached for that golden ring—

quite literally—she'd ended up returning it to Louis.

Trick's presence in Royal had changed her over these last few months—the rumors of his antics had preceded him. She'd gone from a hyperactive, fretting perfectionist to a woman who wore her hair down. A woman who stayed up past her bedtime to make love rather than answer emails.

Unable to stand the suspense, she opened the box. When she moved the tissue paper aside, her eyes filled with tears. They spilled over and ran down her cheeks.

Inside the box was the exact match for the gold flatware she'd been fruitlessly searching for all day. She wouldn't have to wake up early tomorrow after all. She wouldn't have to burden herself or worry about everything matching. As she moved to a back table and set the box onto the waiting folded napkins, she spotted a square handwritten notecard.

In spite of your best laid plans, one issue seems to have worked itself out. ~Trick.

Back in her room, Rylee didn't sleep. She stared at the ceiling, asking herself how a guy like Patrick MacArthur had turned her head. He was her exact opposite in nearly every way. He made no sense. *They* made no sense. Who entered a relationship planning no further ahead than tomorrow? And who accepted an open-ended future without the promise of more?

Hands over her eyes she felt the heat of fresh tears on her palms. A bout of clarity swept through her. Despite her best efforts to prevent it, Rylee, like everyone else who had encountered him, had fallen head over uncomfortable high heels for Trick.

The woman who'd prided herself in having a plan for every possible situation, had never seen it coming.

Twenty-Two

Rylee discreetly positioned herself near the bride and groom as they made their way to an undisclosed entrance.

The guests were making their way to the main entrance, where signs and helpful staff members pointed them toward the reception area. Rylee had checked the room again this morning to ensure nothing had hopped up and run off in the middle of the night. She'd been pleased to find that everything was exactly as she'd left it, but with the addition of fresh flowers from Corynna and her assistant, Hannah.

The blueish purple buds of the blue bonnet were beautifully complemented by the crisp cream tablecloths and shimmering gold accents—including the gold cutlery, a complete set.

The outdoor ceremony had been lovely, and they'd been spared too much heat thanks to clouds blotting out sun. Along with the near-perfect weather, a gorgeous backdrop of mountains and the field of thick, green grass, Ariana was stunning in her bridal gown. On the hanger had been one thing, but seeing the bride in her dress for the first time had been a whole other experience.

Ari, her cropped hair styled and her jewelry understated, had floated down the aisle. The white dress dipped in to accent her trim waist and flared out at the hips. Blue bonnet flowers had been sewn into the skirt but managed not to distract from the bride herself. When Xavier saw her for the first time, Rylee could practically hear him swallowing past the lump in his throat.

Once Ari had reached the end of the aisle and her father had taken his seat, Ari and Xavier hadn't broken eye contact. Even when the officiant addressed them directly, the bride and groom had spoken only to each other.

Ariana Ramos and Xavier Noble had recited their vows. The kiss was the best part of any wedding ceremony, hands down. Rylee had dabbed at her eyes with a tissue, accustomed to choking up during that tender moment. And then the moment had been upstaged by a very young man in a very expensive tux.

The ring bearer had taken it upon himself to leapfrog up the aisle preceding Ari and Ex when they were introduced for the first time as husband and wife. The boy's mother intercepted him and wrestled with the croaking, leaping child. Before Rylee could panic over the ceremony being ruined by the unexpected display, Ari and Ex had thrown their heads back and laughed.

Their reaction had been contagious and had spread to the guests and even the officiant. Rylee had joined them, the stress of the last few months melting away. She'd laughed so hard, she'd snorted, which had made her laugh even harder. At that moment, she'd met eyes with Trick across the aisle, who had been laughing with her. For a prolonged moment, they'd simply stared at each other, grinning like loons.

And then the moment had been over. The guests had stood to follow the bride and groom off the lawn, and Rylee had circled behind the crowd so that she could greet Ari and Ex inside.

She held the door open for Ariana now. Xavier helped his wife with her dress, leaving room for the short train. He made a comment about how the "kid could have thrown in a ribbit or two in order to sound authentic" which made Ari and Rylee giggle over the incident again.

"I guess I'm unable to plan for every possibility," Rylee said.

"Well, it's on video, so we'll play it at his wedding and show him how it feels," Ari said with another laugh. Her buoyant mood was permanent today. "How long until we are introduced?"

"At least ten minutes. We'll give the guests some time to settle in."

"Perfect. One of these gorgeous blue bonnets is tearing loose from my skirt. I know you have a sewing kit on hand."

"I do." Rylee reached into a pocket of her pale pink bag, an almost exact match for her dress.

Ari spun to face Ex. "Could you fetch me a glass of water *husband*? I am parched."

"Sure thing, *wife*." He said the word on a growl into Ari's mouth and then pressed his lips to hers. Rylee busied herself unzipping the sewing kit, the intimate moment stinging more than it should have. Their intimacy reminded her of her own short-lived romance, which had been as unexpected as the ring bearer turning into a bullfrog.

Ex vanished down the hallway in search of water, and Ari rested one manicured hand over Rylee's. Ari's expression was pure concern. "Why are your blue eyes bluer than usual? What's got you down?"

"I—what do you mean?" Rylee slapped on a broad smile. This was Ari's day and Rylee refused to ruin it with her wayward emotions. "Everything is wonderful. Now show me where the threads have popped and I'll do my best to repair them."

"Are you kidding? This is Keely's design. Not a thread on this dress would dare pop without her permission." Ari rested her hands on her hips, looking like the in-charge, take-charge producer more than the demure bride minutes after she'd said *I do*. "Talk to me."

Rylee tucked the sewing kit back into her bag. "Your only concern is to go into that reception hall and be doted on by everyone. Don't worry about me."

"You're my friend. I want you in that reception hall smiling, too."

"I am smiling."

"Like a robot." Ari palmed one of Rylee's arms. "Nothing can ruin this day for me. It's unfolding as it was meant to. Now tell me why you're upset. Is it Trick?"

Rylee debated lying, her mouth opening and closing and opening again before she said, "How did you know?"

"These two eyes." Ari gestured to her face. "And Dee mentioned you two had hit it off. Talk about opposites attracting."

Rylee forced out an explanation that would satisfy any friend. "We spent some time together. He's a good person, but ultimately we weren't cut out for forever. I wish him well, though. He's so talented."

As she waited for the lie to land, her smile faded. That BS would satisfy any friend, except, as it turned out, Ariana. Ari's eyebrows craned upward in disbelief. "Really?"

Rylee dropped her shoulders. "Okay. The truth is—"

"Finally!" Ari raised her arms, bouquet and all.

"The truth is," Rylee restarted. "Trick is good at making people fall in love with him. He is charming and fun, and he has a way of giving someone exactly what they need before they know they need it. Like peach Bellinis, charcuterie boards, a foot massage. Forks." Her vision blurred with tears as she recalled the many, many gifts he'd given her in the last couple of days.

"Forks?"

"Uh, never mind. My point is, everyone falls for Trick. Including you and your husband. I can't trust my feelings when I could very well be part of his shtick." His great-in-bed, feed-her-chocolate, kiss-her-senseless-in-the-hotel-hallway shtick.

"I admit, Trick is likable. I never imagined inviting a wedding crasher to my wedding," Ari said with a headshake.

"I'm sorry. I shouldn't have suggested that."

"Don't be sorry. I was worried for months about nothing. He's wonderful. That interview was from the heart. He can turn it on, for sure, but no matter how great Trick is at his job, it doesn't change the fact that you're wrong."

Rylee's head jerked on her neck. "I'm wrong? About what?"

"I was charmed by Trick. Ex was charmed by Trick. Dee and Tripp were charmed by Trick. Every one of our guests who spoke with him at the rehearsal cocktail dinner was charmed by Trick." She poked Rylee in the arm as she made her point. "But not you. You were the one who *fell in love* with Trick."

Rylee was silent for a beat. She'd been called out. Ari was right. Rylee had fallen in love with Trick. Which was insane, made no practical sense, and had *not* been on the agenda.

"I—That's ridiculous. You can't fall in love

with someone in a few days," Rylee argued. "Plus, he doesn't want to talk about the future. I need to talk about the future. He wants to take it a day at a time, see where it goes. I need assurances that everything will go according to plan."

Ari's smile softened with knowing. "You mean the way everything in our wedding went according to plan? What about when our rehearsal dinner turned into a rehearsal cocktail party with an entirely new menu? Or the color-scheme change or the addition of last-minute guests? What about our ring bearer stealing the show when he became an amphibian?

"There is no way everything will go according to plan, even with a plan as rock-solid as Rylee Meadows's plan. But look at Xavier and me. We're married. As planned! Nothing changed that outcome."

Rylee was beginning to see her friend's point. No matter how firm the plans had been, many, *many* things had changed during the course of planning this wedding. But in the end, it'd all worked out.

"Here you are, sweetheart." Ex appeared with a water glass in hand.

"Thank you, darling." Ari took a sip as the announcer spoke from the other room. "That's us!"

"Meet you in there." Rylee said, taking the glass from Ari, but her friend wasn't done dispensing advice yet.

As Ex positioned himself beside his wife, she whispered, "Remember, Rylee, magical moments happen at weddings."

"Everyone welcome the bride and groom!" the announcer said.

Rylee pulled open the door for them, and Ari's words echoed through her mind. She'd used the word *magical*. The very word Rylee had used to describe Trick.

She silently closed the door on the couple as photos were snapped and flashes popped. Then she looped back to the corridor and slipped in through the front.

As she angled for her own chair, by itself in the rear of the room, her heart lifted. She half expected to find two chairs instead of one, and Trick waiting for her to arrive.

Instead, she'd found the table exactly as

she'd left it. With her planner next to her own set of gold cutlery, and her place card on the center of the dinner plate.

Twenty-Three

The meal was exquisite. Each course came out on time, with every garnish in place. Not that Rylee had checked every plate personally, but as she was positioned near the kitchen, she'd peeked as the servers had whisked by. While she appreciated Colin Reynolds's talent with food, her heart hadn't been into enjoying it. As each course was served, her heart sank lower and lower. Trick hadn't come.

She didn't understand. He'd been at the wedding. He'd laughed. They'd locked eyes. Ariana had pointed out that Rylee had fallen in love, and then had practically promised her a happy ending tonight with that "magical" comment.

During the cake cutting and Xavier and Ariana's first dance, Rylee kept watch for Trick. Ariana threw the bouquet directly to Dee, who caught it with a flourish. Rylee had smiled and clapped along with the other guests, hoping she'd effectively hidden her true emotions. She was a professional, here to serve the bride and groom. Today wasn't about her happily ever after. No matter how badly she wanted one.

Ariana and Xavier were married and enjoying their reception. That had been the goal. Rylee's work was technically done the moment that Dee caught the bouquet, but she couldn't seem to make herself leave. Even as the band played a slow song and warm amber lights swirled on the dance floor.

She watched from afar as Ari and Ex's friends paired up. She kept smiling despite her own empty arms. Her heart ached. Whether or not something magical happened to her tonight was of no consequence. Magic was all around her, and that was a enough reason to celebrate.

Even if Trick had left Royal, Texas, without telling her goodbye.

A member of the waitstaff offered her the lone glass of champagne on his tray.

"Thank you." She accepted the flute. As the waiter zipped away she realized it wasn't *just* champagne. The orange hue exactly matched that of her favorite cocktail.

"Peach Bellini," came a rich, low voice next to her left ear.

She turned around, her heart in her throat.

"Hi."

"Hi," she said, breathless.

"What's wrong? Did you think I wasn't coming?" Trick, dressed in the same navy-blue suit as he'd worn at the wedding, was a literal a breath of fresh air.

"I wasn't sure."

"Well, shame on you. I was invited, after all." He pulled his cellphone from his jacket pocket. "I was wondering if you would take a look at something for me." He swiped the screen. "I've been working hard on it, but it's not quite finished."

"Oh, of course." She swallowed down her yearning and focused on the task. Today wasn't about them. Trick knew that as well as she did. "What, um, what is it?"

"It's a video of those unexpected moments I'm always going on and on about." He rolled his eyes in an adorably self-deprecating manner. "I compiled some for the week, but I wanted your opinion. Unless you're off the clock."

"Have you seen these shoes?" She pointed her toe. She was wearing the gold strappy pair she'd sworn never to wear again. She hadn't been able to resist since they'd paired so well with her dress.

He turned the screen horizontally and played the video. Rylee expected stolen moments featuring the wedding guests to pop up on the screen, but there was only one person featured on the video.

Her.

Trick had filmed her without her knowing. While she had been talking on the phone, or walking around the site. When she'd sneaked a shrimp off a platter at the rehearsal cocktail party when she'd thought no one was looking. He'd filmed her kissing friends hello, and later when she'd hugged them goodbye.

And there were several clips of her slipping off her shoe to rub her sore pinky toe.

"What is this?" she whispered.

"Video evidence of every little thing you did that made me fall in love with you." She looked up at him but his eyes were on the screen. "I have hours of footage."

"Trick..."

"I know. I'm as shocked as you are." He pocketed the phone and offered his hand. "Dance with me?"

She placed her hand in his. He set aside her Bellini, promising that she could finish it later. Then he walked with her to the dance floor and began swaying to the music.

"I thought you went home." She was dazed, her voice hollow.

"Without saying goodbye? What kind of jerk do you take me for?"

"I was terrible to you. I never thanked you for finding the gold flatware. How did you do that, by the way?"

"I can't tell you all my secrets, Peaches. Some mystery is healthy for a budding relationship. And you haven't been terrible.

You've been you. And as I've established, I love you. See? Told you it would work out."

She had to laugh. "Nothing's worked out. There is no pl—"

He pressed his index finger to her lips. "Don't say the *P* word. Besides, I have one."

When he moved his hand away, she said, "You have a plan?"

"I do. I'm going to film events and clip together video montages like the one I just played for you. How does MacArthur's Moments sound?"

"Cheesy," she said with a confused smile What was he talking about? She was still wrapping her head around the *I love you*, and now he was...*starting a business?*

"Yeah. That is pretty bad. I'll poll my fan base and see what they think. They're very smart. Most of them believe that I'll end up marrying the wedding planner I met in Royal, Texas." He shrugged. "I'm not sure she'll have me, but we do have one very important thing in common."

"Wha-what's that?" she asked, her mind tripping over the word *marrying.*

"Coffee. You answered my deal-breaker

question correctly. What more do we need to work out?"

She shut her eyes, information and proclamations coming too fast for her to process. "Trick, what is going on?"

Wordlessly, he let go of her and dropped to his knees. Before she had a heart attack in the middle of the wedding reception, she realize he wasn't proposing, but removing her shoes. He tossed them to one side and stood to applause from the crowd. They adored him—no surprise there. Barefoot, she stood a few inches shorter than him and felt a million times more comfortable.

"Now for a proposal unlike any other. I promise to love you and make a maximum of one plan per month." He faked an eye twitch that made her laugh. "*If* you promise to stop wearing shoes you hate and let me hang around with you on a permanent basis."

"Permanent?"

"Maybe you can tack on my video services as a part of yours? Or if not, I could still join you at the weddings you plan as your date."

"And if you're not invited?" she teased.

"Hmm. I'll find something to do. Do you

know anyone who can teach me how to golf?"

"*No*," she said with meaning. "Do you know anyone who can teach me how to take life as it unfolds instead of planning for every possible circumstance?"

He sucked air through his teeth. "I'm not sure you can be taught."

Her mouth dropped open. "I can so! I've done everything you've asked me to since you showed up in town uninvited."

"That's true. You are a quick study."

She wrapped her arms around his neck and hugged him close. "Do you know what else I'm a quick study on?"

"What's that?" He embraced her, pulling her flush against his body, and making her want to be alone with him as soon as possible.

"You. I have you down. You charm anyone and everyone you meet."

"True."

"You are able to solve any problem with a smile and a conversation."

"Guilty," he agreed.

"And you made me fall in love with you, even though I never planned on it."

Whatever smart-aleck remark he'd reserved never made it out of his mouth. His eyes heated. He dropped his forehead onto hers. "You fell in love with me?"

"I'm afraid so."

"Seems fair. I never saw you coming." His eyes jerked to the side. "Except for the times when I went down on—"

She pressed her lips into his to keep him from finishing that sentence. Then she whispered, "Let's talk about that later."

"Let's go back to your room and talk about it *now*. Are you free, or are there any other unforeseen emergencies you have to circumvent?"

"I'm suddenly free. This great guy I know handled the last of my problems."

"Well, he sounds like a keeper."

She tilted her head and prepared for another toe-curling kiss. "He is. He really is."

Epilogue

Rylee blew out a breath and steeled herself. She'd planned lots of weddings, but over the last year, none had been as significant as this one. She smoothed her dress with one hand and peered into the cathedral where the pews were packed with guests.

"Is it bad luck to see you beforehand?" Trick whispered into her ear.

Startled, she spun to face him. "That rule is only for the bride, not her wedding planner." He gave her a kiss, and butterflies took wing in her belly. "Besides, we don't have bad luck."

"Mmm. Good point." He kissed her again.

"Was this the most challenging wedding you've ever planned?"

"Not even close. That prize belongs to Ari and Ex, and you had quite a bit to do with that."

He raised their joined hands and kissed hers. "Where do we stand for this part?"

"You"—she pushed him toward the side entrance—"go over there and film those unforgettable moments you promised the bride and groom you'd capture."

"What about you?" he asked as he checked the settings on his camera.

"I will wait back here and make sure the wedding party and the bride make it to the end of that aisle."

"So you can head off any disasters before they occur?"

"Exactly."

"Lens check." He lifted the camera and pressed Record. Rylee was used to him asking for her help with lighting tests.

She posed and sent him a cheeky grin. "How do I look?"

"Like a woman who is being proposed to."

Her smile dropped. "Excuse me?"

"We've already combined our lives and our businesses. Why not make it official?" With his free hand, Trick produced a ring from his pocket and extended his arm. "I can't let you continue to be the wedding planner who hasn't planned her own wedding. And I can't bear the idea of going one more month without knowing you'll be part of my future."

"The man who never plans is planning for the future?"

"*Our* future." He lowered the camera, but kept it facing her, the red light on. "You bring out the best in me. You always have. What do you say? Will you marry me, Rylee Meadows?"

"Cliffside wedding?"

"You're the planner. You tell me."

She rushed to him, bypassing the ring to plant a kiss on the center of his mouth. "Why don't we plan it together? I'm flexible."

He grasped her waist and squeezed. "You proved that last night."

Against his lips, she laughed. She liked knowing she'd be laughing with him for years to come. Sometimes the best-laid plans weren't planned ahead.

No matter where they held their wedding: on a cliffside, at the Texas Cattleman's Club or on a space shuttle bound for the moon, Rylee had faith in Trick and in their future. A future that *didn't* have to be perfect.

The best things in life rarely were.

* * * * *

LET'S TALK
Romance

For exclusive extracts, competitions and special offers, find us online:

- facebook.com/millsandboon
- @millsandboonuk
- @millsandboon

Or get in touch on 0844 844 1351*

For all the latest titles coming soon, visit millsandboon.co.uk/nextmonth

*Calls cost 7p per minute plus your phone company's price per minute access charge